Sweet Fatalities

by

Sherrie Lea Morgan

The Heroes of Coweta County,
Book 2

Sweet Fatalities

Cover Art by *Rae Monet, Inc. Design*

The Wild Rose Press, Inc.
PO Box 708
Adams Basin, NY 14410-0708
Visit us at www.thewildrosepress.com

Publishing History
First Fantasy Rose Edition, 2018
Print ISBN 978-1-5092-2138-7
Digital ISBN 978-1-5092-2139-4

The Heroes of Coweta County, Book 2
Published in the United States of America

"It's okay, honey.
The power's gone out. I'll go check the fuse box," Neil assured her with a quick squeeze to her arm.

"No, it's not that. I heard a moaning before the lights went out. Didn't you hear it?"

"No, I didn't hear anything. Likely the wind outside is picking up a bit. We're supposed to have rain tonight. I haven't had time to trim the tree branches."

She shook her head, and her body swayed. He stepped forward, and she wove her arms around his shoulders. He curled his arms around her soft curves and pulled her close, lowering his head to speak into her ear. "I've got you." And he did too. He held her, and he always would, if she'd let him. He sucked in a quick breath at having his hands on her once more.

Hannah's shaking eased, and she mumbled against his chest. His body hardened at the contact. Her lavender scent wafted around and wrapped him in its cocoon. He inhaled and pulled her closer. *Wait*. She'd said something. Her chest vibrated against his, then she tipped her head away. He dipped his head lower to hear.

"I'm scared," she said in a low, trembling voice.

Hannah's next inhalation pressed her soft breasts against him. He bit his lip to stop from groaning and locked his knees. What the heck was she doing to him? His mind jumbled thoughts together when their bodies touched, and now…holding her, he was at her mercy.

Praise for Sherrie Lea Morgan

"*GHOSTDRUMS* [*released 11.30.16*] hits all the right notes, taking you into a story filled with restless ghosts, steamy romance and danger. You'll be rooting for Victoria and Marcus as they fight for a future together, while battling an unseen enemy. Morgan's debut novel is a great start from this new author."

~Jana Oliver,
international bestselling author of
The Demon Trappers® Series

Dedication

This book is dedicated to my daughter,
Heather Lynn,
a woman who has always
encouraged me to keep going.
Angel, I have the string, fly high!

Prologue

Senoia, Georgia

"I'm telling you, boss. The crew is gonna walk." The heavy-set man, in dust covered jeans, spoke over the phone while Muriel floated above him.

"There's no such thing as ghosts," the voice spat through the line.

Muriel smirked.

"You haven't been on site since we started. I've seen some crazy shit, myself, and I'm tellin' you, it ain't pretty," the man argued.

"This project has to be completed in two months. We can't afford another crew."

"If one more freak thing happens, you're going to need more than a new crew. Don't say I didn't warn you," the man snapped and pocketed his phone.

Muriel clapped her hand over her mouth, smothering a giggle. The man surveyed the other four workers who'd installed and sanded solid wood floors in the living room last week. He joined them and started to work on the cabinets in the kitchen. They'd removed all but three of the doors earlier that morning and set them aside.

No such thing as ghosts. Now, isn't he special?

She raised her arms. An ice-cold wind whipped the dust lying about into a frenzy, swirling through the kitchen like a mini tornado—pulling cabinet doors open, then slamming them shut. She released a high-pitched screech which grew higher and higher in volume, bouncing off the walls.

All five men yelled, dropped their tools in unison, and ran to their van. They jumped in and sped away with the wheels spitting gravel—leaving a large cloud of dust in their wake.

The wind ceased immediately, allowing silence to settle. Muriel's misty form danced in the kitchen of the now abandoned house. A feminine laugh erupted as a book fell from above a cabinet and landed on the counter. Pages flipped with a soft, slow, whoosh while the sun cast its light through the windows. Then the laughter faded to sighs.

Muriel DuBois Hanson flipped another page of her cookbook. Hanson House required a manly man's care, someone who would care, not the snobby couple who'd hired strangers to make this house a home again. If anyone found out she'd allowed such a thing to happen... Why it would be quite scandalous.

She'd have to keep tabs, is all. She tapped a perfectly manicured ghostly finger against her chin, as she gazed lovingly around her kitchen. Muriel tipped her head while a smile touched her lips. She snapped her fingers. She'd follow the paperwork. Perfect. Even if it meant she would have to leave Hanson House to investigate. How dare anyone think she'd give up so easily? *Bless their hearts.*

Chapter One

Death by nutmeg?

Hannah gasped, and nine faces turned in her direction causing her face to infuse with heat. She sputtered, "I'm...I'm so sorry."

Heart pounding, she rushed out of the little room and away from her friend Anita and Anita's family. She dodged around monitors, linen hampers, and nurses, blocking out the odors of alcohol sterility assaulting her nose. Why hadn't that nurse warned her? Why had they let her in? Tears pooled, blurring her vision before dripping in rivulets down her cheeks while she pushed forward. Her throat burned as her gaze shifted right, then left, and around the corners she passed, scanning for the double doors somewhere among the maze of the intensive care unit that would allow her to escape.

A bright red button on the wall suddenly appeared to her right. She ran and slapped her palm on the button. She tapped her foot in a rapid tattoo, then stopped when the doors whispered slowly open. Hannah shoved them open farther, squeezing through the opening. Her chef shoes squeaked on the linoleum flooring as she searched for a room, any room to hide in. A trickle of sweat trailed down her back. A small sign indicating a waiting room pointed its arrow to the left. She turned and sank into the first available seat. Lowering her head into her hands, she let the tears flow even harder.

Nutmeg? Did Anita have other allergies that severe? She was a baker, for heaven's sake. *Hello*, pastry chefs used nutmeg on a regular basis. She ran her palms down her face and wiped away the wetness. Her eyes stung from residual tears, and her chest ached from stifling her cries.

An elderly woman's urgent whispers broke through the questions spinning in her mind. Sitting huddled together to Hannah's left, an older man and woman clutched hands tightly—while a nurse knelt before them. All three spoke in hushed tones, words filled with both hope and fear echoed in the nearly empty room with its dim lights. The nurse explained to the couple that their son's car accident had been serious, and the doctor would be with them to explain their child's injuries. The couple bowed their heads in unison and said soft prayers.

Hannah remained still. Their words reverberated in her head, as the acidic burn of bile threatened her throat. Was anyone really listening? Memories of her experience with her own grandmother flooded in. When stuck sitting in this type of room, hope had been her lifeline to keep the fear and darkness from smothering her soul. In the end, it hadn't worked.

She shifted away from the couple and dropped her gaze to stare at the floor. How many people had sat here before trying to make sense out of death? She struggled to breathe as the walls started to close in around her. Since she'd never met Anita's parents before tonight, it didn't make sense to stay. With the other family members arriving, she would be one more in the crowd of bodies trying desperately to comfort those they loved, while at the same time fighting the fear of being too close to death.

As if it was contagious. She clamped her lips together and clenched her hands. The tremors started in her arms, and her breath locked in her lungs, before whooshing out in short gasps. She wouldn't get hysterical. She wouldn't make a scene. *Leave and do it now.* She jumped up, grabbed her purse, and ran down the hall. Like a cold wall, the blaring fluorescent lights of the hospital ceiling stopped her in her tracks. Blinding her after her escape from the dim room. Swallowing the scream fighting to escape her chest, she pushed forward, focusing on the bare colorless linoleum squares leading to the elevators and freedom. Freedom from the oppressing sterile halls filled with human grief and fear.

Hannah arrived at the elevators and poked the down arrow button. She inhaled deeply and lifted her head. She stood alone. No one to witness her panic attack if she lost control. She clenched and unclenched her hands. The elevator chose eons to arrive, testing her. Darn things. The light above the elevator stayed dark.

Come on...come on. Get here already.

The bell marking the elevator's arrival echoed in the empty hall. Her breath whooshed out, and she took a step toward the doors. When they slid open wide enough, she squeezed into the small cubicle, and immediately punched the button for the main floor, then the door-closing button. Main floor...close...main floor...close. Repeatedly she punched the buttons. *Close, close.*

When the doors finally closed, Hannah bent over.

Inhale, exhale. Ding, floor two…*ding*, floor one…*ding*, main floor. When the doors slid open, Hannah rushed out and quickly followed the stark white halls that led outside. Bursting through the exit, she stopped and inhaled the cool, damp, night air of fall. *I guess I'm still not over your passing, grandma.*

Forcing herself to step steadily into the visitors' parking lot, she continued the slow deep breaths, tugging her thin sweater around her, until safely ensconced in her car. She refused to think about what she had just heard, what she'd learned, what she thought. She twisted the volume button on the radio, blasting the interior of her car with bagpipe music. Indulging in the sweet promise of another world to flood her mind with its lilting notes, she concentrated on the job of driving.

The trembling, she'd hope was gone, came back after she arrive home. Hannah finally got her apartment key in the lock after dropping it three times. She rushed into the warm interior. Flexing her fingers and then wrapping her arms about herself, she stumbled toward the couch. Huddling in its cushions, she grabbed her favorite quilt and bundled into the cozy material. She closed her eyes, dropped her head against the cushions, and blanked her mind.

****

The setting sun peeked through her curtains, filtered through her eyelids, and woke her. She'd slept the afternoon away. Drat. Standing slowly, she shuffled to the bathroom. The hot spray of the shower cleansed away the tears and soothed her tense shoulders. Tossing on her favorite T-shirt and yoga pants, she walked back to the living area and flipped on the table lamp. She had convinced her roommate Rose that it added to the bohemian décor.

She poured a half glass of pink Moscato and carried it to the couch. She flopped once again on the cushions, curled her legs up under her, and grabbed her school bag.

Hannah sipped the bubbly sweet liquid, allowing it to cool her throat. She pulled out papers and books, tossing them aside to search more. The list was in here somewhere. Each participant of the annual Elizabeth Sweet chef competition was given a list of the judges and competitors. *It must be here.* Recipes and notes from her baking classes fell out and scattered on the floor. She stopped moving and stared at them. Making a mess wouldn't help—it would only kick her into a cleaning frenzy. *No time. Where is that dang list? Why did Anita mess with nutmeg if she was allergic to it?* Her heart beat a rapid tattoo against her rib cage.

Do something...anything. Stop thinking, dang it. Bake. She'd bake something. *Yes.* She jumped up and headed to the kitchen, leaving her glass among the papers she'd tossed. The repeated steps of measuring, mixing, and handling the dough worked better than any meditation class Rose encouraged her to attend. She frowned, and her shoulders slumped. Rose, upcoming lawyer, demanded meditation classes as a life practice for survival.

"Right. A fat lot of good it did her," Hannah mumbled to no one.

Hannah measured out the half cup of sour cream and quickly mixed it with an egg and a teaspoon of vanilla in one bowl. After putting that aside, she tossed two cups of flour in another bowl. She measured out the third cup of sugar and a teaspoon of baking powder. She measured half teaspoons of baking soda and salt to toss into the dry mixture, then took a moment to clear away and clean the measuring utensils she'd used. "Clean freak," Rose had teased her too many times to count. *Whatever.* The spice raisin scones would work wonders for her nerves. She pulled a box of raisins from the cupboard, poured a cup of those into the flour mixture, and lightly tossed them with her spoon. Reaching over toward the spice rack, her hand stopped inches from the bottle of nutmeg. She gasped.

Nutmeg. She dropped her hand. If she were allergic to nutmeg, the spice would not be in her kitchen. Why did Anita take the chance of using a recipe that called for nutmeg if she'd had such a severe allergic reaction to it? Twenty-somethings surely knew their own allergies. Hannah stared at the nutmeg, and her breath caught. *Wait a minute.*

Abandoning her mixes on the counter, she rushed into the living room and immediately punched on the power button of her computer. She searched nutmeg and scanned the articles. Many teens were now using raw nutmeg to smoke for a quick high. *A nutmeg high?* Too much of it could cause nausea, convulsions, and if a large quantity was taken, doctors termed it a nutmeg psychosis. Hannah blinked, then read more. The psychosis required hospitalization with the adverse effects lasting about three days. Only if injected intravenously could it be fatal. *Injected?*

That doesn't make sense. The doctor said Anita died from an allergic reaction to the nutmeg. Anita didn't do drugs. She'd known that since she met the girl last year when they were in their first Foundations class. Anita's parents were in the middle of a nasty divorce. Maybe she was on some anxiety medication to deal with that, and it reacted badly to the nutmeg, causing symptoms like an allergy?

Hannah inhaled deeply and sat back in the chair, staring at the monitor. It was a freak accident. *Wasn't it?*

Her phone rang and she jumped. Punching the button, she checked the clock and answered, "Hello, Rose."

"Hannah, it's so dark out here. I wish the school would put in more lights. I know I'm repeating myself, but really? Surely a panic post would be smart."

"No, it's okay. You're on the mark, though. It's a good thing I'm here, yes?" Hannah reached for her wine.

Rose's chuckle rippled through the line. "Yep. I don't know what I'd do if you didn't answer the phone. This is stupid."

"Rose, no. It's not stupid. I'd feel safer talking on the phone if I had to walk in the dark to my car too. You can never be too cautious." Hannah sipped her wine then set the glass on the table.

"This is coming from the woman who prefers to be around hot liquids and sharp knives on a constant basis?"

"Hey, it is what it is," Hanna responded.

"Sure is. Hey, I'm here and getting in…again." Rose sighed. "I'm tired of this repeated performance."

"I know. We'll figure it out," she paused tapping her fingers on the keyboard. "Somehow. If I could at least see you—"

"I know, I know. I've tried, but I can't find anyone

9

to ask how."

"We'll work on it," Hannah promised.

"Absolutely. Okay, car doors locked. Talk to you later," Rose said.

"Bye," Hannah replied and scanned her apartment. Her gaze locked on an old grocery list lying on the table. Each item once purchased had been crossed off.

Her breath hitched when a picture of her competitors listing formed in her mind. She jumped up and sifted again through the papers she'd taken out until she found the list. She read through the names. Her stomach churned while a buzzing began in her ears. There were ten competitors with two alternates. In case a competitor dropped out for any reason. Before the weekend break, Chef Patterson informed the group that the two alternates were ill and would not be available to compete. This left the remaining ten. Now with Anita gone, the count was down to nine.

Dang it. I want to win for my skills, not because there's no one to compete against.

No one to compete against… The alternates. First twelve, now nine. How many would remain to actually compete? Could someone… No. *No.* She stood, the paper crackling when her hands shook. She stared at the list where she had crossed out the names of the competitors who'd dropped out.

Hannah shook her head. Slowly, she lowered the list, set it on the coffee table, and trudged into the kitchen. She dumped the mixes into the trashcan and turned off the oven.

"I'm going to school early," Hannah announced to her empty apartment, then spun around and stomped to her room.

After showering, she rubbed on body lotion and focused on getting dressed. She braided her hair in a French braid and neatly tucked it up and under, so it wouldn't fall past her collar. She grabbed the remote and cranked up her stereo. The sweet sounds of bagpipes worked its magic on her nerves while she applied her makeup.

Maybe it would be best to get away from everything and soak up some family time. She'd head home immediately after class. She'd miss the rest of the week. But for a good reason. It was, wasn't it? She could run her theory by her dad and see what he thought. If she was being paranoid, he would be the first to tell her. With her makeup finished, she pulled the small suitcase out of her closet and started tossing in clothes. She carried and placed it near the front door. Picking up the papers she'd dropped on the couch and table, she stopped and reviewed the list again.

Three down, nine to go. A hit list? Get a grip, girlfriend.

Hannah shuddered. She stuffed the papers in her pack and grabbed her newly pressed chef's jacket and headed out. Only after she had settled in her car and driven a good fifteen minutes away from her apartment, did she gasp. She'd forgotten to bring her cell phone charger. Sitting at the stop light, she debated going back. No one would be calling her. Rose had already made her obligatory phone contact. Her parents wouldn't call since they knew she'd be in class. The only other people who might call were from the school. She would be there in about thirty minutes anyway. If it died, she'd recharge it at her parents' house. With that, she proceeded through the light.

****

Across town, Neil Garrett stomped to the refrigerator of his two-bedroom apartment and jerked open the door. Staring at the barren shelves, he grabbed the last bottle of beer. He slammed the door shut with his elbow, popped the cap, and took a long swallow of the cool, crisp liquid. His gaze shifted to the large bulky envelope sitting on the small kitchenette table of his apartment.

"What's that you have there, honey?" a faint voice whispered in his ear.

Neil jerked and shot his gaze around the room. No one there. *Crap.* He shook his head. Exhaustion had a funny sense of humor.

A scent of White Shoulders perfume floated around him. His grandmother and her friends wore that, and after all their hugs, he'd never forget the smell. *But, why here?* Standing perfectly still in the middle of the kitchen, he slowly raised the beer bottle and then paused. Maybe the booze was bad? He checked for an expiration date and frowned. He didn't keep beer around long enough to let it go bad.

"Well, I declare. It's quite rude to receive a birthday gift and at least not open it," the feminine voice whispered again.

Neil stomped to the sink and poured out the contents of the dark bottle. The perfume aroma strengthened, and a cold wind whipped around him. He dropped the bottle and searched the room. *What the hell was going on?*

He rubbed his hand over his face then massaged the nape of his neck. No one ever said turning thirty, then working long shifts in homicide could affect his mind. He finger-combed his hair, causing the waves to go askew, and one dropped across his brow. He swiped it back, then cracked his knuckles. No. *I'm fine.* Just tired. His scowl deepened while he glared at the birthday decorated envelope and ignored the scent of the perfume permeating the kitchen. *Damn it.* That scent reminded him of Grandma and family get togethers. He sighed. The phone call he'd received earlier that day from his Uncle Bruce replayed in his head.

"Hey, kid. She's my sister as well as your mom. We go through this each year that she sends you a birthday present. I'll tell you the same thing this time as all the others. Accept it. Keep it and use it to make your life easier. It isn't as if she wants it. You know, she's tried buying and renovating at least ten houses. Apparently, she gave up on this one. Likely, it was costing her too much." His voice softened. *"My sister or not, I'm the first to admit she's handled this whole motherhood deal poorly. But at least she's not upending your life like she used to do. She's done what you asked and left you alone. Besides, I thought you'd like this year's gift."*

"What the hell am I supposed to do with a house? I already have a place to live," Neil responded angrily.

"It's going to need a lot of work, from what your mom said. I know how much time you spend on those homeless shelters each summer getting them repaired and fixed up. This year, work on something for yourself. Look at it like an investment. Flip it like they talk about on television if you don't want to keep it. But, remember, she never lived in it. It was an investment thing on her end."

Neil could hear the excitement in his uncle's voice

and didn't have the heart to argue. He wouldn't be able to shove this gift into the storage locker he'd rented along with the other gifts she'd sent. Fifteen years of fancy paintings, art pieces, and furniture had him paying a couple hundred a month for a storage unit large enough to hold it all.

"She plays this bribe card every year since she lost custody of me. It's not like it will ever make me forgive her for walking out on me and Dad," Neil said.

"I know, I know."

"I think she caused his death," Neil spat out.

"Neil," his uncle admonished.

"I'm serious. If he hadn't been so caught up with her bullshit—"

"Neil," his uncle said.

Neil sighed, pushed away the memory, grabbed the envelope, and dumped the contents onto the scratchy wooden table as he straddled the chair. Scanning the paperwork, he grunted. *Ah hell.* He glanced at the address. Senoia wasn't far. He spread out the photos of the house and studied them. He whistled as he took in the condition of the house. Immediately, renovation ideas popped in his head. The siding was all shot, some of the windows were broken, and the front wraparound porch was a visitor's nightmare. The broken steps and flooring shouted dry rot. He focused on one picture which showed support beams under the front porch roof. Someone tried working on this before. He snorted. *Loser gave up.*

A giggle echoed in the room.

Neil jerked his head up. *What the hell?* He scanned the room. Dammit, first whispering and now giggling. *Focus.* He glanced down again at the photos.

Best to drive out and take a closer inspection of the place. He blew out a harsh breath. It'd take all through fall and winter, if not longer, working on the weekends. If it was habitable, maybe he'd split habitation and work during his off time to cut the repair time. He picked up the paper with the address and lot information and read the description. Hanson House. His mouth quirked when he read the line describing the Historical Foundation's support of the reconstruction with an immediate disclaimer following it, stating they would not be involved in any rebuilding.

"Oh, absolutely cheer me on, but refuse to help," he mumbled. *Figures.*

Neil put aside the address sheet and shoved the remaining papers and photos into the envelope. It was Monday night, and his twelve-hour shifts meant no trip until after Thursday. First thing Friday morning, he'd head out. He had some time off coming, anyway. He stood and peeled off his black T-shirt while heading to his room, where he dropped his jeans and kicked them into the corner. The shirt followed. Somewhere under the large pile of jeans, socks, black T-shirts, and briefs, his hamper hid. Maybe he should try to wear another color other than black. *Nah.* He dipped his chin. His hamper had to be under there somewhere. *Damn.* Time to do laundry. *Later.*

He headed into the small bathroom and cranked the shower on hot, wincing when the stretch for the knobs pulled on the bandage under his left arm. *Shit.* Trying to jump a barb wire fence was stupid, but those punk kids thought they could outrun him. *Stupid thinking on their part.* The bandage stayed secure, sporting streaks of pink advertising the three gashes he'd received from his jump. *Pfft.* Neil ripped off the bandage and examined the wound. The bathroom mirror reflected puckered but clean stitches. *Good enough.*

Neil stepped in the shower, placed his hands against the tile above his head, and stood under the hot spray. The water sluiced across his back and down his thighs. The heat permeated his skin and loosened his muscles. After a few moments, he moved and washed off the day's sweat and grime, conjuring a list of items he wanted to pack up for his trip to inspect his 'birthday present.' After rinsing, he got out and strode into his bedroom and pulled on clean black boxer briefs, sweatpants, and a tee. He sighed. Four twelve shifts sucked. At least it'd be over after Thursday when the last training conference class ran. Then back to a normal schedule.

Screw it. I'm tired. Short nap, then hit laundry.

Flipping off the bedside lamp, Neil rolled into bed and closed his eyes. A scene from months ago surfaced of a beautiful woman with copper curls streaming over her shoulders and curves that would make a man want hours to explore. She glared at him, green eyes flashing with anger, while her sultry voice speared him with accusations. His body had surged with heat and urged him to touch her. His gut clenched with the need to taste her, and with a frustrated moan, he rolled onto his back. *Not happening. Push it away and sleep.* He ordered his mind to erase the image. His body refused to follow. *Damn it all to hell.*

It'd been too long since he'd been with a woman. He kept fantasizing about that particular spitfire redhead who would just as soon slice him with her cooking shears as kiss him. He'd bet his paycheck that her kiss would be as hot as her eyes. He trembled as the memory returned. Her anger as she answered the questions he'd asked about her nephew sparked his lust again. His breath caught as his body hardened, demanding release. Swearing, he flipped over on his stomach and mumbled against the pillow, "Forget it…forget Hannah."

****

Hannah pulled into the gated lot of the school. When she slid into a marked student parking space, she paused to survey the area. The place was empty even at six thirty at night *Good, still two hours before class.* She'd have time to get some studying done and catch up on emails. She got out, grabbed her backpack and chef coat, and closed the door. She pressed the lock button on her key ring twice. Once the beep confirmed the lock engaged, she dropped her keys into her pants pocket and headed toward the school. *Thanks, Rose, now I'm obsessive about locking the car.*

She pushed the front doors open, and the scents of spices and baked foods greeted her. *Happy place.* She walked down a corridor that led to the library, smiling. The observation windows placed at every kitchen, that allowed visitors the opportunity to watch students and instructors in action, had been cleaned.

Hannah paused at the observation window of her own classroom and scanned the shelving units housing the cooking pots, pans, sheets, and mixing bowls. She then entered the silent room. It would remain empty until her classmates arrived She stepped toward the center area skirting the tall wood-covered workbenches. Under each bench sat empty buckets ready to be filled with sudsy water. All five of the gas stovetops sat side by side on the left, and within five feet of those, along the connecting wall, were six ovens, one on top of the other, like soldiers waiting for orders.

The stainless-steel doors sat two feet high and eight feet long, like a giant steel dresser with flip-up doors for each drawer. Their fronts reflected the bright lights from the ceiling. Across the room from the worktables there were basic ingredients set out for each class. The long ten-foot table would also house the ingredients during the competition.

Hannah approached the table and trailed her fingertips along the wooden surface. Nicks and scratches marred it from knives the students used to cut and chop. She shifted and studied once again the shelving units that hid the extra-large sinks and drying trays. Three students at a time could fit easily in front of the sink when cleaning time arrived. They always bustled to wash and clear out of class for the evening.

Images of Friday night's class flooded in.

Anita stood across the bench and worked her dough for the berry pastries the class had been assigned to create. A few minutes later, she began drying the berries for her dish.

"Hannah, they should do something about these spices. I need to talk to Chef Patterson. We should be allowed to use fresh spices or even raw spices. This bulk stuff goes stale after a few weeks. He should know that. Look at this, the cayenne has a brown tinge to it already!"

Laughing, Hannah quickly glanced at Anita's mixture.

"Go tell him. Refuse to use their spices. We'll go get our own stuff."

"Nah, no time. I'll catch him after class. I hope this doesn't affect the reduction. Using cheap wine and stale spices is going to make one nasty pastry."

Smiling, Hannah concentrated on rolling the dough and cutting it into squares she intended to fold around her berry filling. Her mind stayed so absorbed with cutting the correct size, she didn't register the commotion at first. When the clatter of the pots rang out, someone shouted Anita's name. She jerked around, and her gaze shot toward the stoves. There on the floor, Anita convulsed violently. Dropping her knife on the table, Hannah rushed over and attempted to get to her friend through the crowd of students circling the girl. She reached Anita at the same time as Chef Patterson.

"Move back!" he ordered. Pointing his finger at another student named Wayne, he barked out, "Call 911. Now!"

Hannah's eyes filled with tears when she saw Anita had been jerking her head back so hard it left small blood marks on the floor. Shoving the other students back, she ran for her wipe cloth and returned to try and tuck it under Anita's head. Looking desperately at Chef Patterson, she was shocked to see him so pale. He appeared to be on the verge of crying when he wrapped his big beefy arms around Anita in an attempt to hold her still. Suddenly the doors swung open, and two paramedics rushed in. Chef Patterson ordered all the students into the math lab, except for Hannah and Wayne. He told them to shut down the kitchen and meet him in the lab once they were done. He hurried away with the paramedics and returned within minutes, advising everyone class was cancelled for the remainder of the evening.

****

"Hilly?"

Hannah jumped at Chef Caulder's gravelly voice.

"Chef Caulder"—Hannah spun around and grinned when she recognized one of her instructor's—"How are you doing tonight, sir?" *The name is Hannah. But since you forget everyone else's name, I won't complain.*

"Doing good. Class should start on time, and I need to get the staples out."

"Would you like some help, Chef?" she offered.

"No, thank you. You go on and study. You're still planning on making the plum cake for the competition, Hilly?" he asked without looking directly at her. His voice lowered at the end of his question, as was his habit.

"Yes, Chef, I am—" She turned toward the door. "I'll see you in class," she said over her shoulder.

She paused in her step, waiting for a response. *Nope. Out of sight, out of mind.* Hannah shook her head. He could relay extremely intricate details on the order of mixing or blending whatever dish he was teaching and never forget an ingredient. Yet, he couldn't remember her name. *Who was Hilly?*

Chapter Two

A phone's buzz in the library jolted Hannah from her lessons. She checked the clock across from her study area, gathered her papers and books, and headed to class. Arriving among the other students, she studied the faces of those she had known since her first day of school. After this last round of classes, the head count would start to drop until those who were close to graduation would remain for the final, more difficult classes.

Hannah scooted into her favorite spot among the other students and half listened to their murmurs. Once in a while, she would catch Anita's name spoken in a sad, urgent whisper.

The room quieted at Chef Patterson's arrival. When he faced the students, his voice soft but firm, he made the announcement all of them feared. His confirmation of Anita's passing cemented the knowledge that she was gone, and it wasn't a bad dream after all.

Bless it all. Hannah swallowed several times, clasping her hands in in front of her. Sniffling echoed across the room. She blinked away the moisture and focused on Chef's words.

"As you all learned in your first kitchen safety class, there are many ways a human body can react to various strains of bacteria introduced in the cooking environment. It is not just these forms of bacteria that drastically hurt us. Your kitchen safety class did not go into much detail on allergic reactions. We're not in the medical field. However, you should all be aware that if you have any allergies which you might encounter inside the kitchen, you must make your instructors and administration aware of these allergies. In fact, each of you should have completed that section in your applications."

He sighed and pinched the bridge of his nose. "The school was not aware of Anita's allergy severity until it was too late. The administrator has made it mandatory that each of you stop by the office this week and review your applications to verify the allergy section is current and accurate. This is extremely serious. Those who don't comply risk being dropped from the program. As such, classes are cancelled until next week," he paused and scanned the room. "Any questions?"

When no one answered, he continued, "With that in mind, we will be having the school nurse give a presentation next week on the various allergic reactions we might encounter during our classes and what emergency procedures need to be done if this should happen again. Our next section discusses the Slow Food movement. Does anyone know what I'm talking about?"

Hannah's classmate Wayne Tarnekes raised his hand, showing off the Wiccan tattoos spread over his forearms and wrists. At Chef Patterson's nod, Wayne spoke loudly and passionately to the class. "The Slow Food movement was founded back in 1989. Its purpose was to counteract the global move toward fast food and the theory of losing cultural food traditions..." He continued to discuss the history of the movement.

Hannah's jaw dropped. The 'goth boy' spoke for the first time in weeks. Silence followed his speech, then Chef Patterson pulled papers from his folder.

"Wayne is correct," he said. "I have papers with the address and directions to the Danby Farm. It's thirty minutes away from the school. Monday and Tuesday's class will be held at the farm. They also have cabins which are available for those interested in an overnight stay, free of charge. If you choose to do that, which I'm hoping you'll all do, we'll be picking our own produce and cooking our own meals." He leaned over and gave the stack of papers to the front student. "I'll have a registration sheet after class that you'll need to sign, if you intend to stay."

Another student raised her hand, and at Chef's nod, asked, "Is the overnight stay going to be considered extra credit?"

"No," Chef responded. "As I said, it's voluntary, but an opportunity I hope you'll consider taking."

When the papers arrived at Hannah's table, she took one off the top and passed the stack on. She read the flier, and her lips lifted at the corners. She'd run home, grab her phone, and head over to her parents' house. She wouldn't be missing classes now. The farm was closer to them than her apartment, so she could go straight there next Monday morning. Six days away from everything. Perfect.

Danielle Roberts tapped her shoulder. "You going to stay overnight?"

"Yes, you?" Hannah asked.

"I don't know. I'm getting nervous about the competition."

"What do you mean?" She gripped the edge of her bench.

Danielle bent low and whispered, "The two alternates of this competition were originally considered for competitors. The one reason they got dropped to alternates is they were caught helping each other on a solo presentation. Remember Chef said they got ill and dropped out completely?" She leaned in close, then continued speaking faster. "If they'd stayed as competitors, anyone who had the original listing would see their names listed first…before Anita."

Hannah whipped her head to stare at Danielle. "Are you sure?"

Danielle nodded vigorously. "Totally."

"Coincidence."

"If you say so. I'm not taking any chances," she said before walking out of class.

Hannah remained seated. *It had to be a coincidence, didn't it?* A shudder rippled down her back.

****

The ringing of the phone jolted Neil out of a deep sleep. He grabbed the phone off the nightstand noting the time. He'd meant to crash for a quick nap. *Crap.* His stomach rumbled at him for missing dinner.

"Garrett," he growled.

"Neil, it's me. I need a favor."

Neil frowned at the worry vibrating in the boy's voice. "Tony, how many times I gotta tell you we can't be having these chats. You're a felon now. Lose my phone number."

"No, no. This has nothing to do with me. It's my aunt Hannah, and I don't know who else to turn to. You helped me. I get that. I'm not trying to mess anything up with you. It's just that…dang. Mom and Dad don't even know I'm calling you," he whispered across the line.

The red-headed goddess popped into his head, and he snapped to attention. "What's wrong with Hannah?"

"She hasn't called me in like a couple days. She always calls on the weekends and comes to visit on Monday and Wednesday mornings," the boy said with a shake in his voice. "My probation officer just left, and she was a no show. She promised to be here for each of his visits cuz of Mom and Dad's work schedule. Officer Dickhead wasn't happy that I was left alone. Even though it's not like I'm twelve. I tried calling her first, but it went straight to voicemail."

"Listen, he just wants to be sure you have supervision. I'm sure he understood this first time. If your aunt can't be there, though, one of your parents will have to stay next time. Did you call your grandparents?" Neil asked.

"They can't help, and…well, heck. I don't want to spook them, so I called you. I called Grandma on Saturday, and she hadn't heard from her recently. If I call them again today, they'll get worried too."

Neil recognized the bitterness in the boy's voice. "Tony, take it easy. I'm sure she's fine."

"Sure, sure… I'm not stupid, man. This was a mistake," Tony snapped.

"Watch the tone, son." Neil checked the clock again. "I'm on my last week of four twelve shifts. I'll swing by her place before heading in for work tomorrow. She's probably got stuff going on. If she doesn't show for Wednesday's appointment, I'll kick up the search, okay?"

"Good…good. Thanks. I appreciate it."

"Keep calm and stay out of trouble. I'll keep you posted via your probation officer. Can't have these calls being made or documented. I told you before. Cops and felons can't be friends. It's protocol, and there's nothing I can do about it," Neil warned.

"Okay, fine. Dang, sorry. I'll wait to hear from you," he said, his voice cracking.

Neil disconnected and rubbed his hands over his face. The seventeen-year-old boy still acted like a ten-year-old. He rose and padded toward the kitchen, pausing at the threshold. Nope, no whispering voices or perfume. He exhaled a sigh. Must've been bad beer causing him to hallucinate. Tony's request reverberated in his head.

It was bad enough Hannah invaded his sleep. But now she was going to invade his days, since he had to find her. He grabbed a take-out box from the bottom back corner of the fridge and lifted the lid. He shuddered then pitched it into the trashcan. He searched the fridge and grabbed a day-old pizza slice sitting on the door's shelving. Shoving it in his mouth, he popped open a bottle of green tea and shuffled back to his room. He glanced at the clock. *Too early?* The last time they had contact, she'd mentioned something about being an early riser. That one time he'd almost lost control. *It can't happen again. Get this done and get it done quick.*

Then back to his world…a world without her. *Blast it all.*

Chapter Three

Neil arrived at Hannah's apartment building Thursday morning, and made a beeline to her place upstairs, taking two steps at a time. He lifted his fist to pound on the door but stopped. *Damn. It's five in the morning.* Neighbor's would whine and create havoc if he did that. He gritted his teeth and knocked gently. He waited a few minutes and knocked again louder. He scanned the parking lot. What kind of car did she drive? *Shit.* He'd never checked. He pressed his ear to the door, listening for any sounds inside. Nothing. Three days in a row and she hadn't been home. He'd called Tony's probation officer and confirmed Hannah hadn't been at their meeting yesterday. He clenched his jaw. He had an hour to get into work. So much for a quick confirmation.

He scanned the area. The night's cool air had disappeared into morning warmth causing steam to float off the concrete. No one was out and about yet. He could break in. But if anyone caught him, especially Hannah, there would be hell to pay. She might just be waking up, or worse, in the shower. The images of water and soap sliding over Hannah's curves stirred him.

Neil let out a small growl and stomped back to his car to wait. He wasn't taking a chance of having his imagination confirmed by breaking in and catching her in the shower. No way in this lifetime would he let that happen. *Negative on that.* He called her number and got her voicemail. Perfect. He cranked on his car and left. He'd try again tonight after his shift.

****

Twelve hours later Neil drove back over to Hannah's place. Again, he knocked and again no answer. He loped down the stairs and returned to his car. He forgot to grab dinner on the way here. He eased back the driver's seat and twisted the radio volume to low. Stakeout time without food. Perfect. He'd wait here and confirm all was fine. If he was lucky, she'd show up soon, and he'd have time to get home and finish packing for the weekend.

His gaze focused on the apartment door, and he let his mind drift. A vision of Hannah in the shower slammed back full force from one of his fantasies. Her smooth, pale skin shimmered in the water. Glass doors steamed up as the shower's heat hit the air. Long rivulets of soapy bubbles trailed down Hannah's neck, between her breasts, ran over her belly and thighs to pool on the floor around those pale pink toenails.

He shuddered. Those toenails covered in pink teased him. He shifted in his seat and adjusted his pants. *Damn.* He was hard as a brick. A knock on the driver's side window blasted his fantasy. He rolled his neck shoving the vision away. He stared into the wide eyes of a little blond boy who gawked at him with both curiosity and innocence. *Ah hell.* He shoved the thoughts that lingered at the edge of his mind, switched the heater off in the car, and hit the window button. The cool night air rushed in.

"Hi. Why are you sitting out here?" the little boy

28

asked.

"I'm waiting for a friend. Where's your mom and dad?" Neil asked, stepping out of the car and surveying the parking lot.

"My dad forgot his keys. He's taking me for ice cream tonight."

Neil squatted next to the boy. He must be at least eight, but that made no difference. "Don't you think you should be waiting with your dad and not out here talking to strangers?"

The boy scowled. "I am waiting for my dad. Besides, you're not a stranger. You're a police officer. I remember when you visited before to talk to Ms. Hannah about Tony."

"Yeah, okay."

Silence. The boy stared. Neil stared back.

"Ms. Hannah's not here," the boy announced.

"How do you know that?" Neil asked.

"She left a message for my dad Monday night saying she forgot to make me cookies. Dad said she got real busy. She always bakes me cookies when she goes out of town." The boy crinkled his nose, making the spray of freckles bunch up. "You're not going to arrest her, are you? She owes me some cookies."

Neil jerked. "Why would I arrest her?"

"Because I overheard my mom and dad talking. You're not nice for a policeman."

"Listen, kid." *Why did he feel like he had to explain himself?* "I was just doing my job. Besides, it's my job to arrest people who break the law. If Ms. Hannah didn't break the law, she's got nothing to worry about."

The boy stared at him for a moment. "Did you tell

Ms. Hannah you were sorry for upsetting her? She was really mad at you, too."

"No, I didn't." An idea suddenly popped in his head. "That's why I'm here. I need to apologize to her. Do you know where she went, or when she'll be back?"

"Nope. Why don't you call her? Did you bring her flowers?" He stretched to peer around Neil's car. "My dad always brings Mom flowers when he says he's sorry for being a jerk. Mom always forgives him, and they always end up kissing. Blech."

Neil smiled into the kid's bright green eyes. *Someday, kid, you'll know what that's all about.* "No, I forgot flowers. I better go get some, huh?"

"Yeah, if you're really sorry, you need flowers. But I don't think she'd kiss you."

The curves of Hannah's lush mouth popped in Neil's head. "Oh, that's okay. I'll wait on that part." *Most definitely. That would certainly be worth the wait.*

"There's my dad." The boy pointed to an older version of himself jogging quickly toward them. "He's back. It usually takes him longer when the keys are in his pockets." He smiled at Neil.

Neil chuckled and rose as the man approached.

"Hello. Can I help you?" The man's brow furled, as he pulled his son behind him.

The boy's arm wrapped around his dad's thigh, and he leaned around looking up. "Dad, this is Mr. Neil. Don't you remember? He's here to talk to Ms. Hannah about Tony."

"I'm here to see Hannah." Neil made a point to peer at his watch, then gave the man an apologetic smile. "I got here a bit early, so I thought I'd just wait out here."

"I see." He glanced back at the building. "I haven't seen Hannah since Monday. I think she's out on a school break or something. You might want to call her."

The man was calling his bluff. Neil grabbed his phone and punched in her number. Voicemail. *Perfect.* He lifted his brows at the twosome, ignoring their stares.

"I guess she forgot I was coming by today. I'll try calling her another time." He got back into his car and flipped the ignition key.

On the way out of the parking lot, he glanced at the rearview mirror. The pair remained in the same spot watching him leave. Great. The local father and son guard team. Hitting speed dial, he called up his partner, Brady Lancaster.

"Cast, I forgot to tell you I'm calling out on Monday—depending on the condition of this house and how much I get into it. I'm wanting another day to check it out. Call me if anything comes up."

"Sure thing. I'm working on a few reports due, so don't worry about it. If you want, I can tell the captain you're out checking in with a contact."

Neil sighed. "Nah, I'm not risking anything with that asswipe in charge. I'll go by the book and call out."

"I hear you," Cast responded.

He disconnected the line and drove back to his apartment. Noting the time, he called his long time elderly neighbor, Jacqueline Dane. Thinking of Hannah and her cooking reminded him Ms. Jacquie promised to make a batch of her famous oatmeal cranberry cookies, and he was craving some. Her answering machine kicked on. *Odd.* Ms. Jacquie always got going early and stayed up late. No one wanted to answer their phones today. *Something I should have done.* Since the house, he'd recently acquired, was in Senoia, he'd have to hit the road soon. He'd follow up with his neighbor later.

After almost two hours, one wrong turn, and a pit stop to stock up on drinks and dinner, Neil arrived at the house his mother had given him. The daily heat eased into cool damp air. He parked his car on the side of the house where the concrete had splintered over time and weeds had taken over. The front gravel drive had spread out so much, it was hard to determine where the edges should have been. The pictures he received hadn't done it justice. They must have been taken a couple years ago, since the front porch roof now dipped as if the house had given up and was now pouting at its lack of care.

He got out of the car, walked around, and stood a few feet from the front. Darkness poured out of the dusty, cobwebbed windows. The wind blew dirt across the wooden frames. Missing bolts caused the once bright yellow shutters to hang crookedly. He rolled his shoulders. The weather-beaten siding was warped in various places, and though the front door seemed new, the decorative glass had been hit by something, causing a spider web splinter to spread, marring the clear lattice design.

Neil rubbed his hands together. Cosmetic repairs could be done to make this house look better than any man's castle in no time.

Please let the structural soundness of the place be in better shape. Walking backward, he checked out the roof. No shingles were missing, and the surface was flat. No obvious holes. Looked good so far. He walked around the entire house, examining the exterior and roof line in the light of the bright moon. He let out a breath. A good roof meant the interior had some protection from major damage. The paperwork showed the house had passed building inspection less than five years ago. He smirked. Better have been a reputable inspector.

He turned the corner returning to the front yard. A tarp covered pile of something sat off to the left of the front door. He headed over, lifted the edge, and grinned at the three-foot stack of two by six treated wood boards. His gaze dropped to the porch deck, then back to the boards. They'd left the porch deck boards behind. *Sweet.* He squatted to peek under the pieces of plywood he'd have to walk on to get to the door and noted the porch beams had already been replaced. *Even better.* He rose, taking the key out of his pocket, and picked his way across the front porch, ducking a few splintered rafters.

Neil glanced over and confirmed a support beam had been set up to hold the rafters above. He'd have to fix those soon, or risk hitting his six-foot-four frame every time he entered or exited the place. He slipped the key in the lock, twisting easily until the click confirmed it was open. He repeated the process with the dead-bolt. He spun around, returned to his car, and grabbed his overnight bag, air mattress, tool box, cooler, grocery bags, and a large flashlight. Locking the car, he stepped along the boards, placed a palm against the door and pushed, wincing at the loud, ominous squeaking of the unused hinges. Lubricating oil would fix that.

Once inside, he dropped his bags and smoothed his

hands down his jeans. He'd called this morning to get the utilities activated. They'd advised him, it would take between one and three days before everything could be completed. Should he push his luck? He held his breath, bit his lip, and ran his fingers along the entry wall until they caught the switch. He flipped it up. When the entry lit up with a bright glare, he grinned permitting the air to release from his lungs. *Hot damn.* He stopped and gazed around the place. History and personality permeated this house. Yep, fixing up this place was going to rock. He pulled out his camera, swung the strap over his neck, then jammed the measuring tape and small notebook in his pockets. First, he'd start by taking photos of each room and diagramming the measurements in his notebook. Neil rubbed his hands together when various ideas poured into his mind of ways to complete the work.

In the front left corner of the house, an empty dining area faced the kitchen. It had four large picture windows that opened to an expansive backyard. The recessed lights above shone on the dust covered countertops. He hit a knuckle on the counter and frowned. Laminate? That's got to go, new or not. He swiped his fingers across the layer of dust, and his gaze landed on the stainless-steel double sink. *New sink.* He pivoted and checked out the remaining appliances. All new and stainless steel. And they planted laminate? Had they started to run out of money?

He retrieved his groceries and put them in the huge refrigerator. A good bit larger than the standard ones he'd used. Neil shrugged before scowling at the two ovens sitting atop each other on the right side of the room. Why would someone need two ovens? A gas stove top sat to the right of the ovens, and when he twisted to face the dining room, he found the dishwasher hiding below the island cabinets that separated the two rooms. He tugged open the appliance. The instruction manual sat inside. Never used. He paused staring toward the front door, then dropping his gaze to the floor.

Brand new expensive appliances, solid wood flooring in great shape, and a new door. The seven-year experienced detective inside him popped to attention. His neck itched, and he rubbed a palm across the nape. Why had the prior owners given this place up? The unused appliances could have been returned for cheaper ones. He blew out a breath. Didn't make sense. He shifted and leaned back on the island. The place was his now. Their loss.

He envisioned stained and refinished country cabinets inlaid with glass, wrap-around marble countertops, combined with the existing high-grade appliances. He moved toward the windows and let his imagination spin on. The sun would shine through the windows, sparkling against the stainless-steel fronts.

A vision of a tall, beautiful, redheaded goddess, retrieving cookies from the oven appeared in his mind. When she turned and smiled with luscious, full lips, his body rushed with heated pleasure. Neil inhaled sharply when he recognized the woman. Hannah. *Ah hell.* He blew out a breath. He told the kid he'd find Hannah. Late or not, he'd check Hannah's place again. He growled.

A feminine hum grabbed his attention. He twisted around and caught movement out of the corner of his vision. He froze. On the edge of the counter sat a book.

Its pages whispered as they flipped from one side to another. His jaw dropped, and he squinted. The pages *were* moving. He glanced over, and the windows were closed. He tilted his head and scanned the ceiling. No fan nor air conditioning vent nearby. *What the hell?* He rubbed his hands across his face and closed his eyes. When he opened them, the book sat closed. He shook his head. *Damn twelve-hour shifts.* At least they were over. No more for another two months.

Neil lifted his camera and snapped photos of the kitchen. Shuffling around to the dining room, he took more pictures. The snaps of the camera echoed in the empty house, while he moved to the large room which sat to the right of the front door. He continued shooting photos of the first floor. And then paused near the back door to confirm the same key would open and lock this door as well. Good.

He returned to his bags and after grabbing them, bounded up the stairs to the second floor. There he paused to get his bearings. Several doors greeted him as he investigated the hall, opening every door he passed. The general lay-out of the house settled in his mind. He located the master bedroom containing a connecting bath and walk-in closet, then dumped his bags and the air mattress before heading down and out.

****

An hour later Neil stared at Hannah's apartment building. It was past midnight, and the parking lot was as quiet as a sleeping dog. He had remembered to look up what type of car she drove before arriving. He searched the lot for her car but didn't see it anywhere. Finally, he bounded up the steps to Hannah's apartment and pulled out his picks. Within seconds, the clicking of the lock tumblers stopped, and he opened the door. The bolt wasn't set. *Blast it, why wasn't the bolt set?* Anyone could get into this apartment with a credit card almost as fast as he picked the lock. His heart skipped a beat. If someone got in and hurt her... He growled into the darkness and shoved open the door.

He skimmed his hand on the wall, searching for the switch. He flipped on the lights and paused. Silence. Neil closed the door and began a walk-through, checking for signs of activity. Nothing. He strode toward the back bedrooms, and the first door he opened showed a small bed, desk, and tons of books on the shelves. A few boxes marked *Books* sat open in the middle of the room and filled to the brim.

New roommate's room? Hannah had mention something about having an interview set the day he arranged to question her about Tony. But that was months ago, past time to get settled in. Spinning around he headed in the opposite direction down the hallway to the next bedroom. His pulse picked up when he entered Hannah's room. *Down boy. Think cop.* But when he flipped the light switch and a frilly purple coverlet lay mussed up on the bed, he froze. Hannah's scent hit him in the gut, and his body responded instantly.

Neil clenched his jaw against the lust clawing inside and stomped to an open bathroom door. It was decorated like a typical woman's bathroom with light purple rugs, towels, and bright colored candles. His gaze traveled to the shower, and he remembered his morning fantasy. Without thought, he slid open the shower door, grabbed the shampoo bottle, opened the lid, and closed his eyes as he inhaled deeply. The sweet smell of jasmine wrapped around him. He groaned. The woman was not here, and he was wasting time smelling her shampoo. *Sap*.

Setting the bottle back, he returned to her bedroom, searching for anything that would indicate where she'd gone. On the nightstand, he spied an open address book. He picked it up and read the entries until he found one marked *Mom and Dad*. They lived on the edge of Rome. If she had time off, she could easily make that trip and visit a couple of days. Hannah had probably shown up unannounced and forgot to tell Tony. No, she wouldn't do that to the boy. She was more protective over him than his own mother. *Go figure.*

Memorizing the address, he replaced the book and left. It was too late to drive to her parents' house now. He'd have to wait and head out later. She wasn't going to be happy to see him again. As he pulled out of the parking lot, his heart tripped, and his pulse sped up. Ah hell, who was he kidding? He needed to see her again.

Chapter Four

An hour later, Neil stopped in the gravel driveway in front of Hanson House, then grabbed the blankets, sheets, pillows, and picnic basket he'd stopped to buy at a 24/7 superstore. He lumbered into his now 'home away from home.' He took the stairs two at a time and headed into the master bedroom, making quick work of setting up the mattress, tossing a couple blankets, and one large pillow on the top. The wind outside howled as thunder echoed in the distance. *Storms comin'.* He contemplated the air mattress. Had he put enough air in it? He plopped on his back causing the dust on the floor to stir. No more air needed.

Lying on his back, he scanned the ceiling, pictures of Hannah drifted in and out of his mind. He grunted when his body heated, and the sound echoed off the walls of the empty room. *Damn it.* He rolled off the bed and ran downstairs. The redhead had his mind in such a spin, he'd forgotten to grab his work bag. *Smart move. Leave the gun in the car, idiot.*

A low feminine giggle stopped him on the third stair. He frowned. *No, not now.* He finished descending the stairs. This fixation on Hannah was not helping. Now he'd hallucinated a woman giggling. Damn, he needed sleep. He ran outside, ignoring the cold drops of rain splattering his head and back. Unlocking his car, he grabbed his work bag, and returned to the house. Once inside, he glowered at his now mud-covered boots. *Son of a gun.*

Neil growled, set his bag on the floor, and bent over. Loosening his boot straps, he toed off the offending items. He rolled his shoulders and after moving his bag to the bottom step, meandered around the large living area. The walls had all been repaired and painted a plain off-white color. Tugging out his notebook, he stared at the paper for a few minutes. What did that website say about living rooms? Dark and rich colors would look best with the fancy furniture his mother gave him. He grunted. Dark and rich…sure. Whatever that meant. He inspected the large stone fireplace on the back wall. At least the idiots hadn't painted the stone.

"I do hope you intend to sweep this beautiful floor soon," the woman's voice whispered in his ear.

Neil jumped. His gaze scanned the room finding no source for the voice. Maybe he'd imagined it. He padded in sock covered feet to check out the small hallway that ran under the stairs to the kitchen. The knob on the right side twisted easily and revealed a small bathroom. Nice. The opposite door hid a closet. He arrived back in the kitchen and found a door on his right, revealing a large walk-in closet. No. Not a closet. A pantry room described the area better. Long metal shelving units lined all the walls. A picture of Aunt Kathy's pantry popped into his mind. Her pantry was half this size. Once she caught sight of this room, Uncle Bruce would have one more thing added to his honey-do list.

He swept the door shut, chuckled, then coughed. The dust stirred up with all his roaming had caught in his throat. He opened the picnic basket. Pulling out a cup, he spun around, and turned on the faucet. It sputtered then stopped. No water? He'd had it turned on. He replaced the cup and grabbed a bottle of water from the fridge. Removing the cap, he slugged down the ice-cold liquid while staring at the floor.

Carrying the water with him, Neil grabbed his bag off the bottom step, headed upstairs and aimed directly toward his mattress. He stopped, pivoted, and scooted his feet along the dust covered floor to create a clean trail to the master bathroom, along the sink, shower, toilet, and back to the door. *There. Floor dusted.*

"You can't be serious."

Neil ignored the voice, tugged off his dust covered socks, and tossed them in the corner. He twisted the sink knob. The water poured clear. He returned to his bed, removed his gun from the work bag, laid down, and rolled to his side.

Sleep. Must sleep. House cleaning in morning. He closed his eyes and regulated his breathing, and as his body relaxed, a light, warm breeze brushed across his face. The room was drafty? No. Warm breeze, not cold wind. He clenched his teeth. *Enough. Sleep.*

****

Neil woke to the aroma of bacon and coffee. His mouth watered, and his stomach grumbled loudly. He rolled off the mattress onto the floor, blindly grabbing for his shaving kit. He rose and stumbled into the bathroom. "Come on, man, wake the hell up," he mumbled, making his way to the shower. He cranked on the water knob and waited, eyes closed. *Please let the pipes work.* The water sputtered at first, then sprayed against the walls. *Yes.* He stepped in and yelped. *Blast it.* His eyelids popped open, and his teeth chattered while he reached for the dial. Nothing like ice cold water for a wakeup call. He slapped his palms on the wall and waited while the water heated quickly. He moaned, then washed, while steam filled the room.

Afterward, he got out, dried off and wrapped the towel around his hips. He swiped a palm across the sink mirror. As he lathered his face to shave, the scents of breakfast food wafted in again. His gut clenched and growled for food. He stilled. *Wait a minute. Who the hell was cooking?* He rushed in the bedroom, grabbed his gun, and ran downstairs.

He stopped mid-stride, dripping water, and stared. His jaw slackened at the empty kitchen. He checked the stove and it was cold. A glob of shaving cream plopped on the counter as his hand gripped the edge. *What the hell was going on?* The undeniable odor of a hot breakfast definitely hung in the air. The back of his neck prickled, and he rubbed it. Neil released the counter and stalked the bottom floor, searching for the origin of the aromas. Nothing. No person, no food. His stomach shouted its disappointment with a loud rumble.

Damn.

Neil rubbed his gut and returned upstairs to finish shaving and wash off the grit now caking his feet. *Sleep deprivation. That was it—all it could be.*

After getting dressed, he grabbed his overnight bag and walked toward the stairs. He stopped at the top, gripping the banister. At the base of the stairs, a misty cloud shifted. The early morning sun filtered through the front window and danced on the mist, causing a shape to form. For a few seconds, the figure of a woman appeared then faded into a white shadow. A shadow that floated into the dining room. *Floated?* Neil blinked, then rushed down the steps and into the next room. The odor of food blasted at him again.

The hairs on his neck stiffened, and he shuddered. What in the world was going on here?

"It's not your imagination, nor a hallucination, honey." A southern, feminine voice whispered from across the room.

He blinked and tugged on his left ear. He recognized that voice. It matched the humming from before. This had to be because he hadn't eaten and was still exhausted from work, right? *Right.* He checked the clock.

"You know, I used to make all the meals for the ladies Magnolia Auxiliary Club. Fried chicken, some cornbread, and mashed potatoes would fill your belly sufficiently in the evening. Howevah, biscuits and gravy are divine."

Neil scowled and locked his jaw. His stomach rioted and responded for him, growling its need loud enough to echo off the cabinets. He slapped a hand to his middle.

"There now, see? Your stomach disagrees. You're a good-looking man. I'd say you remind me of my own dear Walter when he was younger. Such a sturdy man."

Okay. Maybe not hallucinations. Haunted? Could the house be... No. *There's no such thing as...don't be stupid.* He shook his head. Just because he hadn't ever experienced it, didn't mean hauntings didn't exist. The minute he denied something was the minute someone would prove him wrong. Not going to happen this time. He'd keep an open mind is all.

"I declare, you are one stubborn man." A soft

laughter floated in the room. "But you'll do. I have decided I will share Hanson House with you. I do hope you intend to marry and have children. I do so love the sound of laughing children. They're our legacy, honey. Remember that."

Legacy? Marry? Children?

Neil shuddered when a picture of Hannah formed in his head. *No. Uh-uh.* He glowered at the cabinets. *It's not haunted.* He scanned the room. Hidden microphones and cameras could do the same thing. He stormed out the back door and turned the corner where the greenhouse he'd seen earlier stood. He scanned the back of the structure. No new or weird wires hung there. Forget it. *A greenhouse, huh?* Pulling open the screen door, he stepped through onto the dirt floor and into a puddle. *Blast it.* He glared at his stocking feet now covered in mud. *Damn it.*

He tipped his head back and scanned the green tinted plexiglass above. No cracks or holes. Where'd the water come from? Scooting around the large table on his left, he met another large table, centered in the room, with plant pots of various sizes. Most were empty, but a few had soil in them. He scanned the wall where several hooks held gardening tools on the side of a cabinet. Why the hell had he come out here? Right, escape hallucinations and find hidden wires and get muddy feet as a curiosity bonus. He placed his hands on his hips. Well, his socks were already ruined, so he might as well check things while already outside.

Neil left and walked around the front before he stopped. A small storage unit sat close to the road on the far side of the front yard. He'd missed that last night. I'm losing it. He made his way over the gravel and rocks. The unit didn't have a padlock. He opened it and laughed. Payday. Inside the unit stood several cans of paint, wood stain, small tools, a circular saw, and brooms. *Sweet.* He grabbed the large dust broom and dug out three large trash bags before going back inside.

At the front door, he dropped and spread one black plastic bag and set his boots from last night on top. He removed his muddy socks and using the broom swept the floor. Neil aimed for the dining room and kitchen first. Once done with those rooms, he stopped, tugged open the fridge, and grabbed one of the sandwiches he'd bought last night. Taking two large bites, he set it on one of the small plates from the picnic basket and then worked his way through the large living area.

In the bathroom, he located a small dustpan and hand brush. Setting the brush in the kitchen, he returned to finish sweeping the hall and entry. The morning sun filtered through the bare windows and splayed its rays across the now clean-living room floor. *Not bad. Not bad at all.* He returned to the kitchen and took two more large bites of his sandwich and washed them down with water. Using the hand brush, he swept off the counters and dumped the dust into the trash bag he'd hooked to his belt while he swept. He returned to finish off his sandwich and checked the time. Another hour before he could leave and head to Hannah's parents house without arriving too early in the day.

Neil worked his way up the stairs and into his room sweeping up dust. By the time he got to the bathroom, a sneezing attack hit him. He splashed water over his face and using the hem of his shirt dried it off. He checked his reflection in the mirror. His once black shirt had faded to a dull gray. His blue jeans, however, still appeared okay if no one noticed his pant leg bottoms were covered with mud splatter. He shrugged and grabbed another pair of socks to slip on.

He picked up his work bag, gun, and returned to the kitchen. He pulled out his computer and did a search of Hanson House. The image of a woman in her forties, wearing a dress that could be from the fifties, smiled at the camera. Next to the woman stood a tall dark-haired man in a suit. Neil peered closer. Son of a gun, that man could be an uncle. An itch tripped down his back. He straightened and read the article describing how this woman was an active member of her community, blah, blah.

He studied her face. It was familiar. He couldn't place it though.

"I'd be more than happy to tell you about myself, if you'd simply ask," a voice whispered in his ear.

Neil jumped and twisted around. Someone was playing tricks on him. Damn Cast and his sick sense of humor. Hiding cameras and microphones in his new house was not going to work. He cleared his throat.

"Whoever is doing this, listen up. Because I'm going to say this once," he paused a moment, ignoring the heat flooding his face. "This is now my property. My house. I will be back in one hour and will inspect every single corner and crack. If I find any of the equipment you've set up to have this piece of fun, I'll tear it to shreds." He scanned the kitchen and stomped to the living room. "I mean it, Cast. It's not funny. You've got one hour to get your electronic crap out of here," he yelled before returning to the dining room.

He'd need new locks. His partner's idea of messing with him like this was a new low. This stunt wasted his time.

"And if I'm still here when you return, sir?"

Neil clamped his lips together, grabbed his keys from the counter, and slammed one cupboard that had swung open. He would not respond. Nope. Not in this lifetime.

"I will not be running...in one hour or a million. This is my home, and you best learn to share it, young man."

All at once the cabinet doors flung open and slammed shut.

Neil took a step back, eyes wide.

"It's all fine, though. I'm willing to share if you behave yourself," the voice sang.

Neil spun around, grabbed his boots, and stormed out. Time to hit the road. He'd be gone longer than an hour, but no one needed to know that.

Pulling out the paper with Hannah's parents' address on it, he punched the information into his phone, plugged it in, and cranked his engine. He spun out, spewing dirt and dead grass behind him. Then an unbidden thought hit him.

What if it wasn't Cast? Shit.

Chapter Five

Hannah took her cup of coffee out to the front porch to join her father. He'd settled in the rocking chair she'd bought for him on his birthday years ago. She stood beside him and laid a hand softly on his shoulder. Tradition demanded she wait and watch the sun break through the morning mist in peaceful silence. Her father had seemed on edge last night, and she hadn't had the chance to talk to him. Now would be a good time to find out what was wrong. After the sun made its appearance, she finally spoke.

"Good morning, Dad." Hannah leaned over and gave him a quick peck on the forehead.

He smiled up at her. "Good morning, sweet pea."

As she settled into the rocker across from him, she studied him. In his early sixties, he was still the most handsome man she'd ever known. "Mom won't say anything, but I can feel something is up. Want to talk about it?"

His eyebrows shot up. "Your mother didn't tell you?"

She leaned forward, and her pulse accelerated. "No, she hasn't said anything. But I've been burning her ears off with my own issues. Why?"

"Issues? You doing okay? Need to run anything by me?"

She smiled at him. "Of course, I do. But you first.

Tell me what's going on."

"Your brother is coming home."

"Oh, Dad, that's great!" Her brother Marcus, had just returned from his fourth tour over in the Middle East. He always visited home when he could, but it had been almost two years since his last visit. When her father didn't smile back, Hannah's shoulders slumped. "Why aren't you tickled?" Her heart pounded when he didn't respond immediately. She gripped his arm. "Dad? What aren't you telling me?"

"He's alive, sweet pea. But he's been hurt."

Hannah gasped. "What? How bad?"

Her father took a deep breath. "Marcus's patrol was hit. The explosion did some damage to his leg. He can walk—or rather, he *will* walk as soon as his physical therapy is up. But he's considered disabled."

Hannah's throat tightened. "And what will happen now?"

Her father raised an eyebrow. "I think you know. They're discharging him. But that's just part of it."

She held her breath. *How bad did it get?*

"Frank was killed, and an investigation determined it was friendly fire from the civilian security group out there. Marcus didn't sound good when we spoke."

Hannah rose and wrapped her arms around her dad. Frank had been her brother's best friend since grade school. They'd both joined the Marine Corps together with plans for the military to be their permanent career choice.

"Marcus has to be devastated. When will he be here?"

"Today," he said with a sigh. "I'm worried about him. I want him to move home. But he's refusing. He spouted off the same nonsense all you kids do about being independent. Like a few years living here is going to ruin him."

Hannah pulled back and looked him in the eye. "Dad, that's your fault for making all six of your kids so fiercely independent. That's why I moved to Carrollton. If he's refusing to return home, then he must have a plan. You know none of us ever do anything without planning it out first."

"I know, I know." He patted her shoulder and waved her back to her chair. "Now drink your coffee and tell me what's on your mind. Worrying about things never gets you anywhere."

She returned to her seat and set the rocker in motion. He needed a distraction, so she told him about the contest, Anita, and her initial reaction when looking at the list. "I know it's a stretch. But, Dad, it seems too coincidental that three students have been eliminated from this contest by either illness or death. I don't know if I'm just being paranoid or what. Besides, I'm not the only one. One of the other contestants approached me yesterday feeling the same way."

Her father nodded and looked off in the distance, as if in deep thought. She waited and gazed out over the front lawn. The sun had burned off the morning steam, and now the once wet grass stretched for the sky. A slight breeze ruffled the leaves of the nearby oak tree that towered over eighty feet skyward. Her mother loved that tree. *One day. My own home will have its own oak tree.*

"Let me stew on it, and we'll come up with something," he said.

"Thanks, Dad," Hannah replied. *Patience.*

Her father rose and entered the house. She sat for a few more minutes before she rose. As soon as she entered, the rumbling of an engine caught Hannah's attention. She stepped back onto the porch. A bright red Mustang moved slowly along the driveway. With the sun reflecting off the front windshield, she couldn't see the driver.

She yelled over her shoulder, "Dad, someone's here."

Her father joined her on the porch, and they both waited for the car to pull up and park. As soon as the door opened, Hannah squealed and rushed off the porch and to the driver. Ignoring the second black vehicle coming up the driveway, she threw her arms around her brother and hugged him tightly. Tears ran down her face as she kissed his cheek, and then leaned back to gaze up at him.

"I've missed you, brother mine," she said, then dropped her head on his shoulder. They stood there, close in their embrace.

****

Neil hit the brakes and witnessed the woman of his fantasies rush toward the male driver of the vehicle parked ahead. She kissed the guy's cheek and wrapped him in her arms. Fire punched his gut and crawled up his body—burning a path to his chest. His muscles bunched tightly, while his fists clenched around the steering wheel. He locked his jaw, and his harsh breath pushed through his teeth. Before he could peel out of the car and tear them apart, an older man rushed off the front porch in a hurried step and joined them. When he drew closer to the couple, his arms enveloped them both.

Great. Just great. She was supposed to be single. She's found some guy already? *Oh hell no.*

Mine.

He forced every ounce of control he had over his body, shifted into park, then sat back. Taking slow, deep breaths, his gaze tracked the trio as they turned and strolled into the house. *Well, son of a gun.* She was alive and apparently just fine. His job was done, duty answered. He could leave now and never come back.

Right, like that was an option. He was going to have to go up to that house and see what type of man could captivate Hannah's heart. It was obvious from their embrace that she cared deeply for this guy. Neil was a glutton for punishment if he pushed forward. But he couldn't leave now. He had to find out. Leaving the car where it was, he walked slowly toward the front door. Although he appreciated the size and obvious well-maintained plantation style home, he preferred something smaller for himself.

A picture of his recent present popped into his head. Yeah, after the renovations, it'd be a little beauty. Stiffening his spine, he knocked. An older woman answered the door. His jaw slackened at the likeness between mother and daughter. She was beautiful, and her eyes sparkled the same as Hannah's.

Instantly a smile crossed his face, and his muscles loosened. "Hello. Mrs. Lincoln?"

"Yes?" Her gaze took in his form, and her slightly creased eyebrows gave away her concern when she recognized him. "Is something wrong…Detective Garrett, isn't it?"

"No, ma'am. I mean, yes, I'm Neil Garrett. But there's nothing wrong. I'm here to see Hannah about a personal matter. Is she available?" Sure, babble away like an idiot. He bit the inside of his cheek, stepped back a pace to make the woman more comfortable, and waited. His stature tended to make folks uneasy.

Apparently having made up her mind about him, Mrs. Lincoln smiled and opened the door. "Please, come in. I'll get you some tea."

Neil followed the woman into the cool entryway, noticing the homemade quilts spread across the back of large, comfortable-looking chairs and a couch. The smells permeating the air were those of a recently cooked lunch. His stomach grumbled. Hoping his hostess didn't hear, he quickly coughed.

She tossed him a smirk and said, "Follow me into the dining room. We're about to eat lunch, and you can join us."

"Oh, I don't want to intrude. I can wait here to speak with her." But the food sounded like the better option.

She laughed. "I think not. Her brother just arrived after being gone several years. The Marines and he just finished a tour of duty in Afghanistan. It's highly unlikely you'll be able to tear them apart. Come on."

Neil rubbed the back of his neck and followed her down the hallway. *Idiot.* The man's her brother. Clearing his mind, he envisioned the man again, and realized he'd completely dismissed the duffle bag the man dropped near his car to prepare for Hannah's hug. He also hadn't registered until he recalled the image, that the man had a severe limp and favored his leg. Some detective he was.

As they entered the large breakfast nook, Hannah sat close to her brother on one side, and the third person of the trio at the head of the table. Her father was smiling, but his eyes bore shadows. *Great.* Family moments were not his cup of tea. This was going to be rough.

"We have a visitor," Hannah's mother announced the obvious, before heading to the kitchen.

Hannah's eyes widened when she spotted him. Her brother regarded him with both curiosity and suspicion. Neil cast a quick glance at the young man and noticed the pain in his eyes before shifting his gaze to Hannah.

"Detective Garrett? What are you doing here?" she asked, rising from her seat.

"Please, don't get up." Neil waved her down. "I didn't mean to intrude. I just needed to speak with you for a moment."

Hannah sat staring at him. "About what? Is Tony okay?" she asked, her voice sharp.

"Everyone is fine. Tony was worried since you missed a scheduled visit with him, and I promised to see if you were okay."

Her eyebrows creased, then lifted. "I called and left a message for him. He didn't get it?"

"Apparently, someone failed to pass on the message."

"Obviously," she snapped.

Mrs. Lincoln arrived from the kitchen carrying a half dozen toasted cheese sandwiches on a large plate. "Hannah. I'm sure Tony will survive. Besides, he knows Mr. Garrett is looking for you." She shot a questioning gaze on Neil. "Don't you agree?"

"Yes, ma'am."

"Good, then sit down so we can eat." She put the plate of sandwiches on the table and headed back into the kitchen.

Neil waited for Hannah's response. At her shrug, he stepped over and sat opposite her and her brother. He grinned at the large plate of sandwiches, a huge steaming pot of soup, and a tray of small cold cuts.

Hannah's eyes twinkled. "Mother believes in eating well, and she hasn't gotten used to not having all her kids at home. Please eat as much as you want, or we'll be forced to stuff ourselves."

Mrs. Lincoln returned with a bowl filled with chopped fruit. Placing it near her husband, she kissed the top of his head and sat across from him at the table, then spoke to Neil.

"So, Detective Garrett—"

"Please call me Neil, ma'am."

"Neil. How long have you worked for the police department?"

"I've been on the force for over ten years. The last seven in homicide."

Mrs. Lincoln frowned. "As dreadful as that must be, I'm sure it's necessary. I understand you were the arresting officer in Tony's case. I should let you know we are a very close-knit family. Tony's parents will be here this afternoon, and they have some very strong opinions on how you handled that case."

Shifting in his chair, Neil nodded. He rubbed the back of his neck. This was worse than being chewed out by Aunt Kathy. "Yes, ma'am, I understand. But it's a requirement of my job to follow the clues, wherever they may lead. Unfortunately, they led me to the guys Tony associated with on a frequent basis. A lot of those guys have rap sheets. The investigation pointed me to Tony. Thankfully, he wasn't the killer we were looking for. However, he did have over five hundred dollars of stolen laptops on him that couldn't be overlooked."

Hannah snorted. "Or perhaps you just wanted to arrest someone. Perhaps you just got overzealous?"

"I rarely make mistakes." Neil's gut burned. "I followed the leads, and they took me directly to your nephew."

"And detective, if you had bothered to take the time to listen to me before, or even taken the time to talk to Tony, you would have easily known he could not have killed anyone." Her voice rose in volume with each word.

"Hannah," her father spoke up.

Neil raised his hand and peered directly into Hannah's eyes. "I did my job as I've always done it. The best way I know how. Sometimes, people are in the wrong place at the wrong time. That's out of my control."

Hannah eyes flashed at Neil before dismissing him and turning toward her brother. "Marcus, how long are you staying to visit?"

Neil jerked. If her eyes shot arrows, he'd look like Swiss cheese about now.

Marcus regarded his sister with low lidded eyes. "I'm only here for the weekend. My discharge came through at the end of last month, and I've answered an ad for a rental in Newnan."

Hannah leaned toward her brother. "Newnan? That's more than three hours away from here."

Mrs. Lincoln cleared her throat. "Newnan is a pretty place and really, closer to two hours away, without traffic. Please let us know when you get settled there, and we'll come for a visit?" Sadness edged her voice.

Marcus nodded. "Of course, Mom." He bent over, rubbing his leg.

This man had some serious pain. His mouth tight, and he grimaced when he thought no one was looking. Neil also noticed the bloodshot eyes and sallow complexion. Marcus was doing some serious dips into the booze. *Just like my old man.*

Neil finished eating and sat back. Directing his gaze at Mrs. Lincoln, he thanked her for the meal and then turned to Hannah. *Kill them with politeness,* is what Aunt Kathy always said.

"I do need to speak with you in private for a few minutes before I take off. Do you mind?"

Hannah shook her head and rose from the table. Dropping a kiss on her brother's forehead, she gestured for Neil to follow her. They moved toward the back of the house into a sitting room decorated with bright yellow paint and crisp white, sheer curtains.

She stood in the center of the room wearing her hot pink T-shirt and matching yoga pants and faced him. "What do you want?"

Now that he was finally alone with her, Neil's mind blanked. Her eyes sparked while she glared at him. She crossed her arms, and his gaze immediately dipped to the full, voluptuous breasts pushing against her shirt. Her eyebrows lifted when his gaze rose to her face. She'd caught his inspection. Heat crawled up his cheeks, and he pressed his lips together. *Crap.* He never had problems around women before. This one tied him up in knots, and he hadn't even touched her. *Ah man. Don't think about kissing or touching.*

"Look," he said rubbing the back of his neck,

"Your nephew asked me to check things out, and I promised him I would. So, now, I want to be sure," Neil explained. He straightened, shoved his hands into his black jean pockets, and rocked on his heels.

Hannah's eyebrows shot up again. "Oh? You have some questions?" Dropping her arms, she stepped forward.

The jasmine scent from her skin enveloped him, and he blinked. Planting his feet motionless on the floor, he locked his legs and his mouth dried when heat speared through his body.

She placed her hands on her cotton covered hips. "What do you have to ask me?"

****

Neil's gaze narrowed, trailing over Hannah's face and focusing on her mouth. Her lips parted, and warmth spread inside the juncture of her thighs. She gasped as heat burned through her body, begging her to move closer. His pupils dilated in response when she leaned in slowly. His hand whipped out and grabbed her arm, drawing her even closer. Her body, inches from his, trembled, and her pulse raced.

"Do it," he whispered, his voice husky and low.

Her lips tingled as her belly quivered. *Kiss him, taste him…touch him*, her body screamed. The corner of his lips lifted, and his mouth opened slightly. *Don't do it.* She shuddered and pulled away.

"No. Now, let go of me," she demanded and tugged at his grip. The sudden release of his hold stumbled her backward. She grabbed the back of the armchair and stiffened. "Don't do that."

His smirk triggered her temper. She spun away from him and took a deep breath, hoping to cool off her body's response. She stared out the window. The afternoon sun had dried the morning's dew from the grass spread out behind her home.

Her father coughed from the doorway.

Hannah stilled, heat rushing up her neck and across her cheeks. She whipped around. "Dad!"

"I brought some iced tea." He glanced at Neil. "I know you said you needed to leave soon, but Hannah mentioned something to me earlier, and I thought she should discuss it with you."

Hannah sputtered, "N...No, that's okay, Dad. It's nothing."

Neil took the glasses from Mr. Lincoln, handed one to Hannah, sat on the nearest couch, and took a sip. Motioning for her to do the same, he waited.

Her gaze switched from Neil to her dad's questioning look. She sighed and dropped on the seat, across from Neil, as far away as the room would allow. "I'll tell you."

Her father nodded and retreated out of the room.

She took a sip of sweetened tea, trying to think of how to explain to him what she thought without looking like a fool while holding down her own libido. This man was trouble with a capital T, and she needed to maintain distance. He exuded sexuality like a second skin, and she had a feeling she would be one in a long list of victims if she allowed it to affect her again.

"There is a competition the school holds each fall. There are over a hundred applications to participate, and just twelve students are chosen. Ten to compete and two alternates. The winner receives a large check to use as the winner sees fit. In most cases, the students participating want to eventually open their own bakeries, and this money would go a long way in helping realize those dreams. Or the student can apply it toward their school fees."

Neil lifted his forefinger. Pulling a small notebook and pen out of his back pocket, he jotted down notes. "What is the name of the competition and how much is the check?"

Hannah tilted her head. "The Elizabeth Sweet Chef competition and why does it matter how much the check is for? It's big enough."

He leaned forward. "It matters, because the larger the pot, the more the risk someone is going to take to get it. Now, how much is it?"

"Twenty-five thousand dollars."

Neil whistled. "That's a nice chunk of change. How much does it cost to go to this school of yours anyway?"

Hannah stiffened. "It costs around forty thousand for all the classes. At the end, you receive an Associates in Baking and Patisserie, and certification as a chef."

"Sweet deal. What would you do with the money?"

Hannah glared at him. "What does it matter? Listen, the reason I'm telling you this is because both alternates have been removed from the competition due to severe illnesses, and one competitor died last week." Her voice hitched on the last word. *Shoot*. She was not going to cry in front of this man.

Neil scowled. "When did this last person first get sick?"

"Her name is Anita, and she didn't get sick, she died. Services are scheduled for Sunday." She pressed her lips together and sniffed.

"I'm sorry. Were you two close?"

"Yes. We're all close. The whole class has been together for over a year now. Only three students have dropped out since my session started."

"Has there been any other issues with students getting sick or dying?"

"No."

"How did she die?"

Hannah took a deep breath. This was going to be the hard part. "She died of anaphylactic shock due to exposure to nutmeg."

"Death by nutmeg?"

She glared at him as her own words boomeranged back at her. "She was allergic to the nutmeg, and too much got into her system."

"Let me get this straight. You've got a baking school where folks go to learn to bake. Isn't nutmeg like a standard thing there? I don't cook, but I know that I've seen that spice name used plenty of times in books and videos for making desserts. Why would someone allergic to a cooking ingredient get into baking?"

Hannah's fists clenched. "Listen, just because you're allergic to one spice doesn't mean you can't reach for your dreams. Anita was a great chef. She was talented and friendly. She helped everyone all the time and would never have jeopardized herself or her life." She jumped up. "This is stupid. Just go and forget I said anything." Tears burned her eyes. No, she would not cry in front of this infuriating man.

"If you need a moment, it's okay. Go on and cry in the other room and get yourself together. Then come back and tell me the rest," he said, his voice softening.

She froze. "Get myself together in another room?"

****

Neil stilled. *Damn.* Just when she might've been warming up to him, he had to blow it with some stupid comment.

"Don't cry," he ordered. *No, no tears. Do anything but cry. I can't handle tears, lady.*

"It's just…between this and my brother…" Her tears pooled, overflowed, and ran down her face.

Blast it. "Listen, I'm sorry. I didn't mean it that way." He jumped up and lifted his arms.

She jerked away from him, her eyes wild. The dam broke with a sob.

Oh no, there they go. The bane of my existence. I'm screwed.

Hannah covered her mouth with one hand and pointed to the door with the other. "Get out," she mumbled behind her fingers.

Ignoring her, he moved and wrapped his arms around her.

"I'm sorry. I'm sorry," he whispered, while her hands pushed weakly on his chest. "Please, stop struggling and let it go. It's okay. I promise I'll check into this. I'll find out what's going on. I'll get answers…the correct answers."

The moment she stopped resisting and her tears seeped into his shirt, he sighed. *Ah hell.* Murmuring words meant to calm, he embraced her, rubbing her back softly, and forced his muscles to loosen. Her scent wrapped around him, warming him like one of his aunt's quilts. Neil's mouth dried as his heart beat a steady rhythm in his chest.

She wept softly against him, and her arms finally wrapped around him, holding on. He stroked her hair and marveled at its silkiness. Dipping his head, he inhaled her scent. His arms tightened. Hannah's body fit perfectly against his. *Damn it.*

Chapter Six

Hannah's pain began to ease. Neil's embrace was gentle and comforting. She wanted to stay in this safe haven. But she couldn't. After that close call with the kiss, she didn't want him to get the wrong idea. If she relented, he'd expect more than just one kiss.

Oh hell, who was she kidding? She was the one who would want more than just one kiss, she'd want more of everything. This man was not the type who would want more than a few kisses, some dates, and one or two nights of passion. Oh man, she could bet they would be hot too. But it wouldn't be enough for her, and with her schedule, it couldn't work. Slowly easing the pressure of her arms, she stepped back. Her body chastised her for its loss of warmth.

"I'm sorry. I didn't mean to lose it and blubber all over you." She winced and shifted away.

When he said nothing, she gazed into his eyes. He raised an eyebrow, and the heat crawled up her neck.

Lowering her gaze, she said, "I truly am sorry. I'm not handling this well. Perhaps I can call you later and give you the rest of the information?" She hoped he would understand. Chancing another peek, she caught a glimpse of a frown on his face before he turned away.

"Fine, here's my number. Call me later, and we'll see what we can do. There's not enough here to file anything formal, but I can check it out on the side. My case load is low now, so I have some time." He handed her one of his business cards where he'd written his personal cell on the back.

"I appreciate it. I do." She cleared her throat. "I'd like to be wrong about this. I hope you know that."

"Well, better safe than sorry. Why don't you give me the list of contestants, and I can check them out in the meantime?"

"Sure, they're in my schoolbag. Let me get it for you." Hannah complied, heading out the room and down the hall. She retrieved the paper from her bag, spun around, and stopped short. He'd followed her.

"I'll leave now and let you be with your family," Neil said standing close.

"No, don't rush off. Stay until after dinner. My mother would never forgive me for shoving a guest out the door without staying for at least two meals. Since most of us kids have moved south of Atlanta, they keep us for as long as they can."

"I've got to make a couple calls and maybe I can do some research on your situation, since we have time."

"We have a small office in the back. No one will bother you," she explained, crossing her fingers behind her back.

"You sure?"

No. "Yes, then you can leave, and I won't feel guilty about kicking you out." She grinned.

Neil laughed. "Sounds good. I'm going to go into the back room and make a few calls now."

"Fine. Just come out when you're done," she said, scoping out how well the jeans hugged his narrow hips before shooting down those long muscular legs. She bit her lip and dropped her lids while continuing to trail her gaze over his retreating body. The hard muscles she'd felt while in his arms, rippled under his black T-shirt while he walked. The woodsy scent Neil wore wrapped around her like a warm blanket. She closed her eyes, inhaled softly and licked her suddenly dry lips. She shivered when her body heated in response. *Enough.*

****

Neil strode to the back room and pulled out his papers, ignoring the tickle down his back. He called his uncle and gave him a status on the house condition, then called Cast and gave him a heads-up on the situation. He asked Cast to run through information on the school, if he had time. His partner complained at the request but agreed to do it anyway.

He caught movement out of the corner of his eye from the side of the house. He peered out the curtains while he wrapped up his call with Cast. Tony's parents had arrived. Tony wouldn't be with them, not with that fancy ankle bracelet, courtesy of the police department attached to his leg. Neil shrugged. Better to be on probation than behind bars. He punched in the number for Tony's probation officer to have him relay finding Hannah. When he finished his call, he brought out his laptop and transferred his notes.

Neil would work in here for a bit, giving Tony's parents time to discover they'd be sharing a meal with him. He set up a search task on the two alternates who'd been taken out of the competition. He also called up an old friend of his from the hospital and left a message asking for information on Anita's death. When he finished, he sought out Hannah. *Like a moth to fire. Idiot.*

He found her sitting in the living room with Tony's parents and her father. Her brother and mother were absent. He stepped into the room and lifted his chin at Hannah. Tony's parents were in front of him, and they had yet to see him. He coughed, and their gazes swung around. Tony's father jumped up.

"What the hell are you doing here?" he demanded.

Before Neil could answer, Hannah's father rose and responded, "He's here to check on some things for Hannah about her school. We've invited him to dinner, Chris."

Tony's father sputtered and spun around facing the older man. "Are you serious, Dad?"

"I am. He is a guest in this house now and will be treated as such."

"He has to leave immediately after dinner," Hannah interjected.

Tony's mother remained seated. Her shoulder lifted, then dropped. Apparently, she didn't have a problem with his presence. If she'd cared more, maybe Tony wouldn't have been involved...no judging. Neil pivoted and stepped toward the kitchen hall.

"I'll go see if I can give Ms. Lincoln a hand with dinner," he said. No way in the world would he stay in this room and deal with family drama. No thanks.

After an extremely stilted dinner, he helped clean up and checked the clock. *Blast it, time to go.* He slipped into the hall and used the restroom. When he exited, he spotted Hannah's brother in the shadows. *That is one hurting man.*

Marcus suddenly dropped his cane and crouched as if under attack.

Ah man. Damn PTSD.

"Whoa there, Marine. It's only me," Neil whispered through the darkness as he stepped closer. He bent down, grabbed the cane, and held it out to Marcus. "Sorry about that. I didn't mean to sneak up on you." Neil's eyes narrowed as Marcus took the cane. "Your sister's worried about you."

"No shit. Just because you're sniffing after her, doesn't mean you need to butt into business that's not yours," Marcus responded.

"Don't be an asshole," Neil said. "It's because I'm putting a ring on her finger that I'm butting in." *Oh hell, where did that come from?* He bit the inside of cheek when his pulse picked up speed. He pushed away the image and focused on the wounded man before him.

"You got something to say? If not, I'm tired and heading up to bed, so get the hell out of my way." Marcus stepped forward to push Neil aside.

"My instinct is to knock some sense into you. But since you're a cripple, I can't bring myself to do it." *Damn, please don't let it backfire.*

Marcus tossed the cane down, grabbed Neil's arms, shoved him against the wall, and leaned in close. "I'm not a cripple, and if you think you can take me on, just try it."

"Yeah. That's what I thought." He swallowed and relaxed his stance. *It worked.* "You're still a Marine, and when it comes down to the wire, you can still make it count." Neil laughed through the chokehold. The weak man still had fight in him. He'd work this out.

"Oh, a demonstration is what you were up to?" Marcus growled and moved in closer until bare inches existed between their faces. "I know what I'm capable of… Do you? I doubt that very much, cop, so back the fuck off." He stepped back.

"Sure. I'll back off." Neil tugged down his shirt. This guy had no idea how much fight he still had in him. He smirked. "You'd be faster if you backed off the booze. You do realize that isn't going to help. Liquor's worse than that cane you got there. Besides, I don't want any drunks at my wedding."

Dammit, there it was again. Neil's stomach clenched. *Stop it.* Hannah wearing a wedding dress flashed through his mind. His gut clenched as though Marcus had punched him. He waited until Marcus headed upstairs, took several long breaths, then sought out Hannah. Time to leave before he started spewing those words out loud in front of Hannah. She'd really be pissed at him then. What on earth was he thinking? They'd only known each other for less than a year and most of that time, she hated him. Then again…she couldn't hate him too much judging by her reaction to him earlier.

He stomped through the house until he found her in the kitchen…of course. Isn't that where all chefs hang out when they're at home? *Idiot.* He stopped and observed her for a few minutes. Marriage? He waited for the usual stomach clench that normally followed when using that word. Nothing. Weird. He rubbed the back of his neck, then straightened, before entering the kitchen. "I need to head out," Neil announced. "I have some things to do, but I'll be available after nine. Call me then."

****

"Tonight?" Hannah's stomach fluttered, and her pulse raced. *Tonight?* "I have plans later. I can call you tomorrow night or after Anita's service on Sunday," she offered as she walked him to the front door.

"I'll be available tonight and tomorrow night. You afraid to call me?" he challenged her.

Her chin rose. *Yes.* "No. I'm not. I'll call."

"Good." His wicked eyes glinted as he grinned. "Tell your family it was nice to meet them."

Hannah studied Neil while he sauntered off the porch to his car.

"He's handsome in a dark, mysterious kind of way. If he wasn't a police officer, I might be worried," her mom said from behind her.

She shuddered and slid a glance at her mother. "No. We're not going there, Mom. I have plans for my future, and I don't have time for anything like that now."

Her mother's attempt to appear innocent failed.

"I'm serious, Mom. Please." She wrapped her arm around her mother's shoulders in a quick hug. "Not this one."

Her mother sighed. "Not even a quick fling? I bet he'd be hot in bed."

"Mother!" *Oh god, I bet he would too.*

"I'm old but not dead, honey. I saw the way he looked at you."

Hannah gaped at her mother and blinked. "No, we are most definitely not discussing this, and you're not old."

She closed the front door and guided her mother back down the hall. They'd walked a few steps when her mother stopped. "Baby, do you think your brother is going to be okay?"

"I don't know, Mom. I think he needs time to figure things out. We'll give him a bit." She leaned in and whispered, "You know me. If we don't see results soon, I'll be after him."

Her mother clucked her tongue. "I know how close you two are, so I'll leave it to you. It might be too much if we all gang up on him. Please let me know if your father or I can do anything, will you?"

"Of course, Mom." Hannah leaned back and smiled. "Don't forget how stubborn I can be. That brother of mine won't have a chance."

****

Saturday afternoon, Neil arrived at his apartment to grab another change of clothes to take to the house. He unlocked his door, then glanced across the hall. Normally, Ms. Jacquie told him if she was going out of town. It'd been almost a week without any word from her. Two or three days, he wouldn't bother. His gut clenched. *Something's wrong. Damn it, he shouldn't have waited so long.*

He knocked on his neighbor's door. No answer. Spinning around, he rushed into his place, grabbed the extra key she'd given him, and returned to her apartment. He knocked again. Again, no answer. He pressed his ear against the door. Nothing. *Screw this.* He unlocked the door and edged it open. No radio…no phone chatter…no television. *Quiet. Too quiet.* Sweat trickled down his back. He lifted his gun out of its holster and clasped it close to his thigh.

"Mrs. Dane? I need a cup of sugar," he called out. Slipping into the living room, he checked the kitchen and breakfast nook. No signs of any recent activity. Standing still, he listened. Silence.

He prowled from room to room in the small two-bedroom apartment taking only minutes. His heart

71

pounded when he noticed nothing out of ordinary for an eighty-nine-year-old lady. Holstering his gun, he flopped in her sitting chair in the living room and flipped open her calendar. There was nothing noted for the week she'd been missing. *Damn it.* He rose, planted his fists on his hips, and scowled. At least he hadn't found her lying on the bathroom floor.

Neil bent over and breathed heavily as his stomach rolled. Where was she? Where did she go? Did someone take her? Was she hurt? *Blast it all.* The shrill of the phone ringer made him jerk around and stare at the answering machine. Did that thing still work? Pushing the volume up, he listened to the caller's message.

"Jacquie, where are you? This is my third message. If you don't call me by tonight, I'm calling your neighbor and the police." The caller sighed and disconnected the call.

That had to be one of her pinochle friends. Quickly closing and locking her door, he returned to his own place, flipped open his cell, and started calling hospitals.

****

Neil strode down the hallway of Rockford Hospital, and cringed at the smell of disinfectant mixed with other odors frequently found in a geriatric ward. Blast it all, he should have checked on her sooner. Three doors down, Ms. Jacquie hollered, and his heartbeat slowed. The woman was in rare form, arguing with some poor underpaid hospital worker. He waited near the door, grinning.

"Get your hands off me!"

"Mrs. Dane, please. You can't leave without seeing

72

the doctor first. You took quite a tumble last week, and we need to make arrangements for home health care." The orderly was sweating and flushed from his failed attempts at corralling the feisty woman back to her bed.

For her age, his neighbor was light on her feet and a spitfire. He had known her for the last six years, and she never lost a fight. The orderly was in trouble.

"There you are, Ms. Jacquie!" Neil rushed forward and nudged aside the orderly to give her a gentle hug and kiss on her forehead.

"Thank God you're here! Get me out of this place. They're going to kill me."

"Absolutely. I would have been here sooner if you had called me in the first place," he admonished.

A blush crept up her frail neck.

He kept his hand on her shoulders and faced the orderly. "I've signed the necessary paperwork. If you'll get the chair, you can take her to the front, and I'll be there with the car."

The orderly nodded quickly then fled the room.

"Ms. Jacquie, where are your bags? Let's get you out of here."

She scowled at him. "I don't have anything. Since I fell at the library, they dragged me straight here, and I haven't been off their stupid drugs long enough to make any calls."

"Let the orderly wheel you down to the entrance. I'm going to get my car." Pausing at the door, he nodded toward her bandaged foot. "How long are you supposed to be off that foot?"

"Six blessed weeks!"

He grinned. "Okay, one week down, five to go. You're moving into my place until your time is up."

Her eyes widened, and her fists punched her hips.

Neil kept talking to keep her from arguing. "That's not up for negotiation. My place or here, your choice." He planted his fists on his hips, mimicking her, and raised a brow.

Her eyes narrowed at him while at the same time they twinkled. "Your place, then. I knew you'd figure out some way to get me there."

Neil laughed and wagged his brows. "But of course. Now I'll have you all to myself."

An hour later, Neil carried his neighbor into his apartment. With her weighing less than a hundred pounds, he didn't even break a sweat. He set her on the couch, handed her his phone, pad, and pen. "Call your answering machine and return messages so everyone stops worrying about you."

"There's just Sheila. I'll call her."

Neil's jaw slackened. He planted his fists on his waist and glowered. "What do you mean there's just Sheila? I thought you had plenty of other friends that you visit and do whatever you do with." He sighed when she just sat there looking frail and refusing to answer him. "Fine. Call Sheila. Did you get dinner in that place?"

"No. You going to cook me something?"

He laughed. "Nope. I'm going to call delivery. You got your choice of Chinese, Italian, or pizza."

"Chinese sounds great," she replied.

Neil pointed to his phone. "Give your friend a call, and I'll order us some food."

While she made her call, he grabbed some pillows and a blanket out of the guest room, then pulled the footstool around so she could set her foot off the ground. He placed the blanket on her lap. She gave him the phone and tucked the blanket around her more securely.

"You okay for now, or do you want to take a nap while we wait for the food?"

"I'm comfortable here." She leaned her head back and immediately began snoring.

Neil studied her. Her skin, thin as tissue, showed bruises around her arms where the hospital must have taken blood. Shaking his head, he got another small blanket to place over her. While she slept, he cleaned up, visited her apartment to grab her daily medications, and packed a small bag of overnight clothes. She needed to be comfortable, even if it was at his place. Double checking to be sure he didn't forget anything, he quietly entered his own apartment. She was still sleeping. He glanced at the clock, loped into the kitchen to boot up his laptop and make some calls. No work at Hanson house until Monday. *Fine.*

Half an hour later, Neil leaned back, stretched his arms over his head, and worked out the kinks in his shoulders. He rolled around all the information gathered so far in his head. It seemed like Hannah was on to something. After reviewing the curriculum, he confirmed that all students were taught throughout classes the uses of various foods, spices, and ingredients to make their dishes. But the instructors also included multiple warnings of misuse. As cooking students, these folks should not have made the mistakes they made to get sick...or worse, dead. All victims had a connection to this competition. *Why were the competitors being eliminated, and by whom?*

All remaining competitors were suspects. He blew

out a breath. *Even Hannah.* If any other cop landed this, they'd come to the same conclusion. Hell, he couldn't afford to go down the wrong path on this one. It was obvious Hannah was still pissed about his last case involving her family. She hadn't called last night like she said she would. He rose and checked on Ms. Jacquie. Her snoring filled his living room. Good.

He grabbed the Chinese pamphlet menu and placed their dinner order. Then he was back on Hannah's problem. He would have to get inside the school and check out the other students. Also, he needed to know who had access to the classrooms. And he would have to do all of this without making anyone suspicious. It was too late to pose as a student. Besides, without more evidence, it was unlikely the school would allow him free rein to investigate their students.

Neil pocketed his cell phone and grinned. There was one surefire way to get access to the classrooms and not draw too much attention. *Hannah won't like it. Pfft.* If she wanted help, she'd have no choice but to go along with him. He glanced at his watch. He'd fill her in when she called tonight. She'd call too, especially after getting the message he'd left earlier calling her a chicken. The woman was too stubborn to admit he made her nervous. *Good.* She made him itchy...more than itchy. Her temper acted like an aphrodisiac to him. *Go figure.* She was trouble. He frowned as he gathered his notes and laptop and stuffed them in his work bag. Trouble had become his middle name lately.

An hour later their food arrived, and they ate together on the couch, while Ms. Jacquie caught him up on what happened in the library and the ensuing ride to the hospital. He cleaned up, and she took her medication. He fixed her an icepack and got her leg propped up on the stool. Once she settled back on the couch with a promise to holler if she needed him, Neil took the plates and trays into the kitchen for cleaning. But first he made sure Ms. Jacquie had the television remote nearby.

After finishing, he checked on his neighbor before heading to his room for the night. She'd fallen to sleep again while watching her after-dinner shows. She'd likely sleep until morning, knowing her habits. With his door closed, he settled against his headboard and waited for Hannah's call. He frowned. He never waited for a woman to call. His imagination took flight, and images of Hannah's body up against his had him hard in minutes. Damn, that woman was hot.

The buzzing of his phone interrupted his fantasy. Neil grinned at the display. *Stubborn woman.* "I started thinking you weren't going to call, again."

"I almost didn't. I just got back home," she replied.

Neil glanced again at the clock. "Your apartment building's security sucks, and you wait until nearly midnight to get home with everything that's going on?" His blood boiled. "You have classmates getting hurt, and you're traipsing around in the dark?"

She inhaled quickly. "I'm not stupid, Neil. I've lived here several years and know the area. Besides, the accidents have been happening at school not at homes. I'm safe."

"You're safe." *Sure.*

"Yes. Listen, I'm in my apartment. I made it from my car just fine."

"In the dark with nothing anyone could remotely consider as security. Good to know." *Damn it.*

"Is that what this phone call is about? You criticizing me on my safety, or do you have anything else to talk about? Did you even look at my paperwork?"

"Honey, I have lots of things we can talk about. But since it's late…right now, we'll talk about your situation."

"Fine, talk."

Neil grinned at her exasperated tone. She hadn't said not to call her honey. *Progress.* Could he get her to talk about other things? His body tightened at the idea of doing some late-night sex talk.

"Hello?"

Her voice shook him. *Man, oh man.* "Yeah, I'm here." He coughed. "Listen, I reviewed the list and your notes. I did some checking on the side. You might have something here. But for me to get a good feel of what might be going on, I need to get inside."

"Inside? You mean as a student? It's too late to register for the class."

"I know that. And it'd take too long to get the admin approval to pose as a student if we want to see what's going on now."

"I agree. So, what do you propose?"

He paused and took a deep breath before continuing, "You've had Tony come visit you at school in the past, correct? I'm betting all the students have friends, family, etcetera come visit from time to time during and after class, yes?"

Hesitation hitched her breath before she answered, "Yes."

"Okay, I'm your new boyfriend."

"What?"

"Boyfriend. It'll give me a good reason to hang around the school during classes and afterward. You can introduce me to everyone, and I can get a feel for things."

"Don't you think posing as my boyfriend is a bit extreme? Why not my cousin visiting from out of town," she suggested.

"Honey, do you think I could pass as one of your relatives?" His question met silence. He wanted her to agree to his plan. A part of him *needed* her to agree. She took a deep breath. "No, you wouldn't pass as a relative. Fine. Boyfriend. Fine."

"What time should I pick you up tomorrow?" Neil asked.

"For what?" she asked, and sounded pissed.

"For class. I'll be taking you to class and waiting around until you're done, so you can introduce me around."

"No classes until next week."

"Why not?" *Yeah, sure. Keep saying that and maybe you'll convince yourself.*

"I have Anita's services tomorrow. Look, if we're going to be convincing, we can start with that. If you're going to act like my boyfriend, my friends will wonder why you didn't go with me. Pick me up at nine."

"Nine. Good. I'll be there." He grinned. Dropping his voice to a deep whisper, he asked, "So, what are you wearing?"

Chapter Seven

"What? No. I'll see you tomorrow," Hannah retorted.

Neil chuckled as she disconnected the call. *What was she wearing?* She checked her clothes. Thin sleep shorts and a tank. So not sexy. What was *he* wearing?

"Not going there," she mumbled and climbed into bed. Unfortunately, her mind refused to cooperate, and immediately envisioned Neil stretched out on a large bed wearing nothing but boxer briefs. *Black. Yeah, bet he wears black.*

It'd have to be a big bed. One of those California king-sized ones since he was so tall. He'd probably made sure his bed was big enough to stretch out in. Heat curled inside her belly. She didn't have time for this. She truly didn't. She closed her eyes and inhaled deep. When she exhaled, her body relaxed. The vision of the sexy cop whose voice would melt chocolate led her to sleep.

****

The next morning, Hannah finished dressing and peeked in the room that belonged to Rose. She'd have to pack everything up soon. Her phone buzzed, and she answered it.

"Hannah, I got a response from your cousin Debbie," her mom said. "She's searched all over Eden Prairie and even drove out past Minneapolis. No one is carrying plum baby food."

"Dang it," Hannah returned.

"Have you tried writing to the manufacturer directly?"

"I've done that. They haven't responded."

"You sure you want to use this recipe for the competition?"

"Mom, it was Great Grandma's personal recipe. So, yes, I do. I've got all the ingredients except for the baby food. It's going to win the contest, I know it."

"I know it, too. But I've been to more than ten stores on this side of Atlanta, and I can't find plum baby food anywhere."

"That's the key ingredient. I've checked online and nothing. If I can't find it locally, I guess I could try to make it myself."

"Make baby food?"

"Yes. No, not really. Make a plum puree. It's better than nothing."

"True. Well, I'm still waiting to hear from Diane. I don't think she's going to find anything in upstate New York. But at least we're trying."

"True. I'm heading to Anita's services today. I'll touch base with you later, okay?"

"Of course. Love you," her mom said.

"Love you, too," Hannah answered before tapping the disconnect button. She frowned.

Shoot. Between Marcus, Rose, and now Neil, how could she concentrate on getting anything done? First things first. There had to be someone she could find to help Rose.

Hannah stomped to the living room and checked the time. Neil would arrive soon. Perhaps he could help? Yeah, sure. Help her like he helped Tony. Her stomach churned, and she pressed her fingers to her temples. Pain pounded behind her eyes. She rolled her head to ease the stiffness in her neck. She'd figure it out…somehow. But how does one search for a ghost psychologist? Take out an ad? Do an internet search? *Ugh.*

The knock on the door made her jump. She took a deep breath. *One thing at a time.*

She opened the door and gazed into the eyes of the man who had invaded her dreams last night. Her heart tripped a beat, and a zip of tingles skittered across her skin. Instead of burning, her stomach now had a dozen miniature whisks twirling and tapping and tickling her. Her mind blanked for a second before she realized her body leaned forward slightly. She pulled back and smiled. "Let me grab my coat, and we can go."

"Sure thing," he responded with a grin and stepped inside.

She put on her coat, and the room spun as Neil grabbed her and pulled her to him. Before she could sputter a word, his lips were on hers. Hot pressuring lips. She gasped, and his tongue delved into her mouth. Hannah wrapped her arms around his neck and kissed him back. He tasted of sweet cranberries and oats. *Cranberries?* His flavor filled her mouth, as the woodsy scent of his body wafted around and warmed her. His kiss gentled, and he pulled away.

"You looked like you needed that," he said.

Hannah stared at him. *Wow.* She was tired of fighting right now. She grinned.

"I did. Thanks. Let's go," she said, ignoring the widening of his eyes.

****

Neil's lips quirked as he followed Hannah out of her apartment. When she'd opened the door, she looked so lost and sad, he couldn't stop from reaching for her. What was it about this woman that made him act before thinking? *Danger, quicksand ahead.* Then again, sometimes danger could be fun. He chuckled and followed her to his car.

When they arrived at the graveyard, Neil parked, then circled the car, and opened Hannah's door. The gray clouds of September bloomed across the sky, making the crisp, soft wind nip at his skin. He buttoned his coat and waited for Hannah to tighten the dark purple scarf around her neck. The stark contrast of the scarf against creamy skin made him pause for a moment. *Oh man, she's beautiful.* Then he laid his arm around her shoulders and walked with her to the service site.

"Why are we starting at the grave site? No memorial service?" Neil whispered.

"Because of her age, her parents only allowed immediate family members for the main service. It was a very short service."

Neil grunted, then tracked the gathering of people shuffling to stand stoically against the cool day. Their gazes remained downcast as if avoiding seeing the brown shiny box sitting above the rectangular hole in the ground and why they were there. He frowned and searched the faces of the few who did look. Some had grief plainly written on their features. Pinched brows, tears, and downturned mouths contrasted with those whose eyes were filled with curiosity. Like watching a train wreck. There was always a sparse representation of those who could not, *would* not, avoid attending a funeral service for sheer morbid curiosity.

He accompanied Hannah to near the edge of the crowd and maneuvered her so he could have a good view of the attendees. Who might be there to celebrate this loss of life?

Hannah's shoulders shook, and he glanced sharply at her. She was crying. *No. Not the tears again.* He pulled her tighter against him.

"Lean on me, if you need to," he whispered.

She nodded, and the tears continued to trickled down her cheeks. The droplets as well as the wind reddened her face. Neil's chest tightened, and he swallowed past the lump in his throat. How did this woman affect him so much? *Focus.*

"Do you recognize everyone here?" Neil asked.

Hannah's head jerked, and she surveyed the crowd. She nodded. *Great, no strangers.* Whoever did this had to know everyone else. *Shoot.*

When the pastor began speaking, Neil tuned out. One funeral was pretty much the same as others. At least this one wouldn't involve a 'last radio call' which occurred for police officers. Those services about killed him. He focused on the crowd and the mourners. His gaze stopped on one young man in the back of the crowded clump of young adults. The young man he noted, looked around as if bored by the services. He dipped his hand into his jacket and pulled out a cell phone.

Texting during a funeral? *Dude's an ass.*

Neil altered his position to get a better look. The man in his sights had hair to his shoulders, and the edges of tattoos poking out from his coat cuffs. Black jeans, black coat, and a black shirt made up his outfit. Neil focused on the kid's face and memorized his features. He'd make sure Hannah introduced them before this was over. He needed a name.

When the service ended, the crowd converged into a line-up mumbling their condolences to Anita's parents, whose faces were blank. Lips formed the words of thanks for each person who gave their apologies. When it was Hannah's turn, she gave both the parents a quick hug. Neil stepped back as she spoke with them in hushed words. A small light flickered in Anita's mom's eyes for a moment before blanking out again when Hannah leaned away.

Before they arrived at the group of students standing off to one side, an older gentleman stomped up to Neil. Hannah didn't notice and kept walking toward the students. Neil waited and jerked when the man grabbed his arm.

"Who the hell are you?" the old man demanded. His eyes flashed fire.

"Excuse me?" Neil asked. What the hell? He lifted the man's hand gently, but the old fart had the grip of a younger man. Neil tightened his fingers around the man's wrist and twisted. The man gasped and released his hold.

"I asked who the hell are you, and watch your hands, or I'll sue you for assault."

"The name is Neil Garrett, and I happen to be a police officer. I doubt you could get me for assault since you grabbed me first, old man." Neil took a step closer, and the man's eyes widened before he stumbled back. "You want to tell me your name?"

The man sputtered then swallowed. "I'm Chef

Caulder. I'm worried about my students, and Hilly didn't look comfortable with you."

"Hilly?" Neil looked around and caught Hannah's eye.

She frowned and rushed to join them. "Chef Caulder," she said lifting her arm across the old man's shoulders. "Are you okay?"

"Who is this man, Hilly?"

"Chef, this is my boy…boyfriend, Neil."

"Boyfriend?" Chef Caulder said, and the creases on his forehead deepened. "You have a boyfriend? No, you can't have a boyfriend. Not now." The older man faced Neil. "You leave her alone!" He swung and planted a punch on Neil's cheek.

****

Hannah gasped.

Neil stayed extremely still. His voice dropped low. "You're going to want to walk away now, sir."

Uh-oh. Hannah stepped forward and stationed herself between the two men. "Chef, please, calm down."

She placed a hand on Neil's arm. "He doesn't realize what's going on sometimes." She swallowed and spun around to Chef Caulder. "Sir, it's okay. You're upset and tired. It's been a hard day for all of us. Do you have a ride home?"

"Yes, of course. But Hilly…you can't have a boyfriend. There's too much going on right now."

What did he mean? Chef Caulder never commented on her personal life. Until now, of course.

People started to whisper, pointing at them. The school's dean strode their way.

She wrapped her arm around the man's shoulders

and began guiding him back to the parking lot. "Chef, I know what you mean. Here, let me walk with you a bit."

"Okay, okay. I just want to protect you, Hilly."

"I understand. But I'm okay."

"Dr. Sullivan said to take charge. So, I'm taking charge of things. Nothing will go wrong this time."

"This time?" Hannah frowned. "Who is Dr. Sullivan?" A chill, not from the wind, scratched the back of her neck. She shuddered.

"My doctor. Ever since my wife died, I've been seeing someone to help me through the grieving process."

"Oh, that's a good idea." *Wait a minute.* His wife died five years ago. "It never hurts to get help. I hadn't realized things were still so difficult for you. The hurt never goes away. But, I hear it weakens with time."

"What? What are you talking about? It hasn't been that long." He shook his head. "Never mind. It doesn't matter. I'm free now. Free to make sure everything works out now."

"Excuse me, Chef Caulder?" Dean Hampton said.

Hannah stopped walking. *Oh, shoot.* She turned and grinned at the dean. His dark skin contrasted sharply against the tight white curls of his hair. His voice still carried the deep Cajun drawl of his home in Louisiana.

"Hello, Dean. Chef is still upset about today, so I was helping him to his car."

The dean studied her and then the man next to her. "I'll walk him to his car, Hannah." He stepped forward, "John, let's get you home."

Chef Caulder dropped his head and nodded as they

walked away.

Oh, man. Hopefully, everything would work out. She shook her head and inhaled deeply. The cool air filled her lungs as she headed back to Neil. She pasted a small smile on her face upon returning. The other students corralled around her.

"Is he okay?" one student asked.

"What was that about?" another student chimed in.

"I've never seen him get violent before."

Everyone spoke at once.

Hannah lifted her hands. "Listen, he's just a bit confused, and I think Anita's death hit him harder than we thought. He'll be fine, I'm sure." She asked Neil. "You're okay?"

Neil grimaced. "He's an old man and didn't have much weight behind that punch. I'm fine." He lifted an eyebrow. "Want to introduce me to your friends, honey?"

Honey? Hannah pressed her lips together. *What goes around comes around.* Hannah slipped her arm in Neil's and faced her friends. "I want you all to meet my boyfriend, Neil Garrett." She grinned. "Neil, pumpkin, meet my friends."

His arm hardened the minute the endearment danced off her lips.

After she made the introductions, Hannah bit her lip to hold back a giggle. *Gotcha.*

By now, the crowd had little to say and began leaving. Neil stepped forward and held out a hand to the man in black he'd noticed earlier.

"Nice to meet you…?"

"Wayne…Tarnekes," the guy said softly. "Sorry, I gotta run."

Hannah studied him for a moment before heading toward Neil's car. Neil caught up with her.

"So, you want to tell me about the old man?" he asked.

"He is truly a nice man. He lost his wife around five years ago and took some time off work. He returned this year and is an excellent instructor," she told him.

"What's with him calling you Hilly?" Neil asked.

"I'm not sure. He's lucky to remember anyone's name and rarely uses titles. Ever since he returned, though, he's taken to me, and he keeps calling me that name. I don't know why. But since I seem to be the one person whose name, for lack of a better word, he remembers, I leave it be."

Neil cranked the car. "Something else is off."

Hannah blew out a breath. "Why are you so suspicious? For heaven's sake, he's old. He lost his wife and is trying to get back into society. Give him a break."

"I'm gonna have to follow my gut on this," he said.

"Really? The infamous gut that told you Tony, a seventeen-year-old boy was a killer? That gut? Excuse me if I'm not impressed." *Drat him.* He pushed her buttons in a way she couldn't ignore. And to think she'd kissed the jerk. She clenched her hands, letting her fingernails bite into her palms.

Neil's eyes widened before he faced forward and peeled out of the lot.

"It's a graveyard, Neil. Show some respect," Hannah bit out as she slapped her hand on the dashboard and pressed back in her seat.

Her supposed boyfriend let off the gas and slowed

to a stop near the exit.

"Sorry," he snapped.

Yeah right, he's sorry. Sorry he agreed to help her. Sorry he drove her here today. *I bet he can't wait to get rid of me now.*

Chapter Eight

Two days later, Hannah stood next to her car staring blindly across the lot. She unlocked the door, got in, turned on the engine, and drove away. She blinked away the tears as they streaked in a steady stream down her face. She didn't wipe the water that trailed down her neck, across her chest, and stained the front of her shirt. The class had returned early from their farming trip. The trip had gone well, and despite the announcement Chef Patterson had just made, she wanted to do the trip again. But now, her stomach burned, and her chest ached like a serrated spatula scraped the insides.

Her phone rang, and she hit the speaker to answer.

"I figured I'd have to leave you a message. You're back early. How was the farm trip?" Neil asked.

"Great until now," she responded. How did he know exactly when she returned to town?

"What do you mean?"

"We got back to the parking lot about an hour ago, and Chef Patterson told us he'd received notice on the trip back that another student has died."

"What? Where?" he asked.

Hannah sniffed and blinked her eyes. "Belinda Peters. She doesn't go to my school, but a lot of us know her."

"How? Wait, let me meet you at your place, and

we—"

"No. No, I want to be alone." Hannah blew out a soft breath. "Belinda graduated last semester early. She was one of the competitors, Neil." Hannah trembled and sniffed. "That's four down, eight to go. I don't know what's going on, and I don't want to think about it. Belinda was an awfully sweet girl. That's all I know."

"You don't know how she died?" he asked.

"Oh, sure. Yeah," Hannah snapped. "See, the thing is Belinda has a peanut allergy. That's why she focused on alternative-flavored desserts. Somehow, she encountered peanut oil and had a severe reaction…severe enough that she's dead." Her voice rose an octave. *No.* "So, that's that. Goodbye." She punched the power button while keeping a tight grip on the steering wheel. She swiped at the tears pouring down her cheeks and ignored the trembling of her lips while she inhaled short quick breaths.

Hannah cleared her throat and focused on the road, blanking her mind of everything but two words. *Get home. Get home.*

****

Neil glared at the phone and threw it across the office. *What on earth just happened here?*

"Hey, watch that throwing arm there, Garrett," Cast said as he picked up the phone and tossed it back.

Neil caught it deftly and shook his head. "There's a mess going on, and it's getting worse."

Cast dropped in his desk chair and swiveled around.

"What's up?" he asked.

"Not our case," Neil said.

"Since when has that stopped you?"

Neil laughed. "True and it's gotten me in trouble before, too."

"True. But since Captain Asswipe got transferred, you might be able to get away with it."

Neil frowned. "What happened with that, anyway? How'd we get so lucky? That's why I don't take too much time off. Things get missed."

Cast snorted. "Well, somehow our glorious captain was at an award function without his wife, and next thing you know, he's caught by Coweta County in a van full of hookers. His transfer was approved within twenty-four hours."

"Hmm…and somehow, someone knew he was in a van full of hookers?"

"Well, I heard it mentioned he'd had too much to drink at that dinner." Cast shrugged. "That's all I'm saying I know."

"Uh-huh. 'Kay. Well, then, do we know who his replacement is yet?"

"Nope. But whoever it is, the lieutenant said they aren't due to start for another two weeks." He leaned forward, pointing at Neil. "That means we've got two weeks to figure out this new problem of yours. Who caught the case anyway?"

"That's the thing. There isn't a formal case filed. I've got a file here with all my notes and shit I've researched. I don't have any evidence to prove it's a valid case. I can't go to the boss with conjecture." He tossed the file to his partner.

"Damn, and no one's connected the dots yet?" Cast asked after flipping through the file.

"Not all the competitors go to the same school. I

don't know." Neil responded.

"Well, then, I'm in."

"Yeah, thanks, man. But if we can keep it between us two for now, I'd appreciate it. Less people poking, less chances of it getting reassigned. Get my drift?"

"Got it," Cast said.

Neil spun around and searched the computer files for the specifics on Belinda's death. She'd died up in Fulton County yesterday. One day after Anita's funeral. "Is Julien Jordan still working in Fulton?" he asked out loud.

"Yep. Nope. He quit last month is what I heard," Cast responded.

"Quit? Why? He was our best cold case detective ever," Neil said. That man had talent.

"Heard tell, he solved too many cases a little too easily," Cast said with a shrug.

"What the hell does that mean?" Neil asked.

"Superiors pressured him on releasing his sources. He told them to screw off, then up and quit." Cast swiveled in his chair and stared out the window. "I don't blame him."

Neil frowned at his best friend and partner, then spoke, "You planning something I should know about?"

"No. Just getting tired of it all, ya' know? If I had Jordan's kind of family money, I'd be gone in a blink," Cast said in a low voice.

"I don't get tired of it. Each day is a brand new shiny butt kicking day for me." Neil laughed. "One more chance to put a bad guy behind bars makes me smile like a kid with hot cookies."

"True that," Cast said. "Ignore me." He tossed Neil an address book. "In there is Jordan's personal cell.

Call him. Even if he's not on the force, the man has a way of finding out things."

Neil tilted his head. "I worked with him a few times. Seemed solid to me. What are you not saying?"

"He's 'gifted,' " Cast said as he motioned the quote marks with his fingers.

"Gifted?" Neil asked.

Cast shrugged. "I don't ask. He don't say. I prefer it that way, and you would too."

Neil grunted and punched in the number.

"Jordan," the man answered.

"It's Neil Garrett from Coweta County, you got a few minutes?"

"Hold on," he said.

Julien yelled at someone in the background. "Wait your turn with the rest of your lot." A door slammed, then Julien spoke, "What's up?"

"Listen, I need some information on a case Fulton caught."

"I don't work there anymore. I have my own P.I. business now."

"Cast told me. But don't you have anyone you can hit up for information? I've got no contacts there."

"I've got contacts everywhere, but not the force."

"Shit."

"What kind of information you needing? I might still be able to get it."

"Oh yeah? How?"

"You sure you want to know? Cast didn't give you the scoop? Most partners chatter like gossiping hens."

"Did you and your partner act that way?"

Julien snorted. "Nope, he didn't want anything to do with me."

Neil straightened in his chair. Should he ask? "Why?"

"Ghosts, man. I see them. I don't care who knows now, because I work in the private sector. You got a problem with that?"

Ghosts? Like in Muriel, the meddling old lady ghost? Neil gritted his teeth. *Nope. Not going there.* He cleared his throat.

"Nope. I don't care how you get the information. I'm in a tight spot now. How much you charge?"

"You got a new house recently, eh?"

Neil's jaw slackened. "How'd you know?"

"Don't ask. I got a gift heading your way. You let her do her thing there, and we'll call it even. I like spreading the joy."

"What kind of thing?"

"Dude, you want my help or not?"

"Yeah. But, I don't understand why you want to give me a gift in exchange. Makes no sense to me."

"It'll help my business. That's all you need to understand."

"Fine," Neil said.

"Give me what you have, and I'll get back to you as soon as I can," Julien promised.

Neil gave him the details he had on Belinda. A few minutes later, he hung up. "Gonna go do some legwork. And you're correct. Julien Jordan has an uncanny way of finding out stuff. He's gonna call me later." He grabbed his case book, tossed on his coat, and marched out of the office.

A few minutes later, he pulled out onto the main road, and the scene from the funeral filtered in his mind. Hannah with tears in her eyes, her body shaking with grief. He'd caught that same tone in her last call. His stomach burned, and his chest tightened like he'd gotten caught in a vise. *Damn it all to hell in a handbasket.* He checked his mirror, flipped the car around, and headed toward Hannah's place.

Just going to check on her and be sure she got home okay. That's all. Nothing else. Neil growled. *Keep saying that, and maybe you can convince yourself.*

He slammed on the brakes once he entered Hannah's apartment complex parking lot. His hands gripped the steering wheel so tight, his knuckles whitened. His heart kicked into overdrive at the blue and red flashing lights, at the patrol car guarding the base of the stairs leading to Hannah's place. In seconds, he jumped from his car and sprinted up the stairs. The door opened, and a policeman stepped out.

The officer held up his hand, and Neil halted. "You can't come in here. Please return to your apartment."

Neil yanked out his wallet and flashed his badge at the officer. "What the hell is going on here?"

Hannah stepped around the patrolman and stopped in front of him. "Neil?" Her face, pale as a winter sky, lifted.

His legs weakened, and he locked them before speaking. "Good thing I decided to swing by. You okay?" He shouldered past the uniform to prod Hannah back into the apartment.

She nodded. "I'm okay now, officer. Thank you for coming out so quickly."

Neil slammed the door in the officer's face.

"Neil, stop that, it's rude," Hannah said, trying to shove past him.

"He's fine. Now—" he tugged her down with him

on the couch and lowered his voice—"sit, please." When she complied, and leaned to place her head on his shoulder, he swallowed. *Damn, this is bad.*

He laid his cheek against her hair, which smelled like lavender and sugar cookies. It caressed his face. The tightness in his chest eased.

"Tell me," he ordered.

She shuddered and told him about hearing someone trying to get into her apartment.

****

Hannah inhaled Neil's scent. The woodsy aroma reminded her of a forest. It wrapped around her like her grandmother's quilt keeping her warm and safe. She leaned into his embrace and rested her head on his firm chest. His beating heart sped up, and her muscles relaxed a bit. At least she wasn't the only one affected so strongly.

Why him? When he ordered her to tell him what happened, she couldn't keep her mouth closed. Words spilled about the attempted break-in. She bit her lip to keep from telling him she had punched in his number first before coming to her senses and calling 911.

Independent or not, she wasn't stupid. No way did she plan to stay here tonight. Not until she at least got the locks changed and a security bolt installed. She glanced at the clock. *Shoot, almost time for Rose's call.* As if on cue, her phone rang.

"Don't get that," Neil told her.

"No, I have to." She grimaced when he frowned, and she hit the answer button. "Hello, Rose, how are you doing tonight?"

Their routine call played out as it normally did.

"Okay, car doors locked. Talk to you later," Rose

said.

"Bye," Hannah replied and shut off her phone.

"Your roommate?" Neil asked.

"Yes. She calls nearly every night, and I made a promise to always answer." Ever since that first time, Hannah could never ignore her call.

"Where is she?" Neil pulled out his cell phone. "I can have someone walk with her at night to help her feel safer."

"Oh, no, that's okay. Besides, that's a waste of manpower. She calls me every night on her way to her car. It's fine." She held her breath until he powered off his phone, then gave him a small smile. "It's our routine."

"I see," he said.

She mentally crossed her fingers. She looked around the apartment...her once safe place. "I'm not staying here tonight."

Neil stood. "Of course, you aren't." He waved toward her room. "Go pack. We'll wait for your roommate. What's her name?"

"Rose, and we don't have to wait for her. She won't be home until early morning."

Neil's forehead wrinkled. "If she has a man, how come she doesn't call him?"

"She doesn't have a man, Neil. She goes out to eat with friends." Hannah crossed her fingers behind her back. *Not going there now.*

"I can have a uniform watch the place," Neil offered.

"No. It's fine, okay? Besides, I have a late appointment tonight, then I'll go check in at a hotel."

"What? No, you'll stay at my place," he said.

"What? No, I am not staying at your place." *No, no, no. Too much temptation.*

"Fine. I'll take you to your appointment and then over to a hotel."

"Neil." She sighed. "I'm a grown woman. I can take care of myself." Hannah waved her arm. "I'm smart enough not to stay here tonight until I strengthen my locks. I can get a hotel room on my own too." She blew out a breath, crossed her arms, and stared at him.

Neil stomped over and stood within a foot of her. He leaned over until their noses almost touched. *Don't look at his mouth. Don't look...don't... Shoot.* Her gaze dipped and locked on his lips. Memories of his kiss danced along her skin. She forced her gaze back up, and his eyes had darkened to a deep chocolate. She stood still and bit her tongue to hold it in place. Her lips screamed to be licked.

"You'll be safer at my place." His breath caressed her face. Her heart beat a tattoo inside her chest. "I can't," she said, then swallowed and stepped back.

He grinned at her.

Curse him. She whipped around and shot for the door. "I have to go. You can let yourself out. I don't care." She rushed out and down the stairs. *Curse him for making me run.* She ignored his pounding feet behind her, quickly hit the unlock button to her car, jumped in, slammed the door shut, and hit the locks. Ignoring him, she cranked the engine, and peeled out of the parking lot. *Racing away like a child.*

She inhaled and exhaled several breaths before easing her foot off the gas pedal. No need to get into an accident. Hotel rooms sucked, but she refused to act like she'd already become a victim. Besides, he'd jump at the opportunity to seduce her again. *No way.* An hour later, she pulled into the school parking lot, and after locating a space near the entrance, got out and traipsed in. The nurse was due to meet with each of the students tonight and review health risks.

She pressed her fingers to her temple. Her head pounded like a restaurant full of clattering pans and glasses during a happy hour. Maybe she should drop out of the contest. It could extend her life. But she wasn't allergic to anything, so she should be okay…shouldn't she? Her feet slowed as she approached the classroom door. Her happy place had turned into a nightmare. She shuddered. She could do this. She *would* do this. *My daddy didn't raise no chicken.* She chuckled. *Yep, cautious but not dumb.*

Forty minutes later, Hannah walked out to her car. Short meeting filled with form corrections, adjustments, and clarifications for the administrator. Thank goodness that was over. She checked the time. Marcus had responded to her odd request of ghost hunters. She blew out a breath when she read the referral to his landlord and didn't ask for details of her request. Good. The image of her family floated in her mind. They'd have demanded to know why she wanted ghost hunting contacts. Marcus never let her down.

As she clipped her seatbelt, she looked out across the parking lot and sighed. The hotel would be lonely and quiet. She didn't want to be alone. Neil's offer echoed inside her head. Could he be trusted to behave? It would definitely be more comfortable to stay at his place than a hotel room. She could concentrate on some homework too. She'd make him a meal to pay him back for permitting her to stay. A trade-off would work, right? *Right.*

Her body warmed when she made her decision. Did he have the essentials in his kitchen? Could she cook a meal there? *Like she needed those answers.* Her body scolded her. He might misbehave. *She* might misbehave. She trembled. *But misbehaving, might not be so bad.*

****

"Ms. Jacquie, I got the bed made up for you. You'll be a lot more comfortable in the guest room, than on that couch," Neil said when he joined her in the living room.

His neighbor's favorite show had just ended, and he intended to get her settled. In case Hannah changed her mind. A steady warmth filled his body when he imagined her in his place.

His place. *Crap.* He scanned the area. Clean. Good.

Ms. Jacquie patted him on the arm. "I'll see you in the morning."

Neil leaned over and pecked her cheek with a quick kiss. "Sleep well."

She hobbled into the guest room and shut the door. He paced the floor, and after two laps around the couch, he stopped short. What if Hannah wanted to sleep on the couch? Or worse, what if she wanted *him* to sleep on the couch? He removed a cushion. No one would be expected to sleep on a couch with a missing cushion. No. Too obvious and stupid. He tossed the cushion back on the couch. His body hummed like a smooth song as the image of her in his bed shimmered in his mind. His bed. His arms. *Damn it.* He adjusted himself and stomped to the kitchen. *Screw it.*

A soft knock on the door made him jerk. He

slipped it open to see Hannah standing there. Immediately, his body tightened. The scent of lavender and vanilla wafted in and surrounded him like silk. He inhaled deeply and smiled.

"Hi. Wasn't sure if you were going to take me up on my offer."

"I bet," she responded with a frown. She raised both brows. "You going to make me stand out here?"

"No, no. Come on in," he said and lifted a finger to his lips. "We have to keep our voices down though... I have a guest—"

"What?" Hannah spun around. "I'm not staying here if you have your girlfriend here too. I'm too tired for that kind of scene."

Neil grabbed her arm and stopped her from leaving. "Whoa there, honey."

Hannah pulled her arm out of his grasp. "Don't call me honey."

"Listen, will you?" He scowled at her. "She's in the guest room and will be in there all night. She's recovering from an accident, okay?" His stomach churned at the sight of her leaving. She *had* to stay. But still, she jumped to the wrong conclusion too fast. Not good.

"So, I'm to stay here with you and your girlfriend—"

"Not girlfriend," he said. "Yes, she's female and she's a close friend."

Hannah crossed her arms, took a deep breath, and waved at the closed door. "Just tell me if she's going to cause a scene when she sees me."

"No. She won't. She's very nice, and I think you'll like her." Damn it, she was a spitfire. And those eyes when they shot sparks caused his heart to pound, and his body to harden painfully. A scene involving kissing played in his head. His breath shortened.

Her eyes widened, and she pointed at him. "No kissing," she ordered. She shimmied past him and dumped her bags on the couch. "If you'll give me a pillow and blanket, I'll crash here. I'm super tired."

Neil ground his teeth. *Uh-uh.* Garretts didn't give up that easily. He relaxed his shoulders and forced his lips to lift. "I just put Jacquie to bed, so I didn't have a chance to get the couch ready. I'll sleep there, and you take my room."

"No," she snapped back. "I can sleep on the couch."

"No," he responded. "I don't let ladies sleep on the couch when there's a perfectly good bed available."

"It's not available," Hannah said.

"Don't argue," Neil ordered as he walked over, picked up her bags, and stomped to his room. He dumped them unceremoniously on his bed, spun around, and stormed out.

She stood next to the couch with her arms crossed.

"If you're still standing here in one minute instead of in my room getting ready for bed, I'm going to kiss you whether you like it or not."

Hannah gasped and took one step back.

Neil growled as he stalked to her. "Too late, honey." He swept her into his arms and captured her mouth with his. His hands stroked her back as he tilted his head to take the kiss deeper. His mind blanked except for the taste of her, the feel of her body against his, the scent of her filling his nose. Her soft curves pressed against his chest and stomach. His body roared for more, and he tightened his arms. His body tensed, waiting for her to push him again, then relaxed the second her hands grab his hair, and returned his kiss.

She opened her mouth, and he delved in for more. Her tongue danced with his. They fell onto the couch, her body collapsing against his, and his body sang with pleasure.

Hannah's hips pressed against his, and he hardened even more painfully. He shifted to place her under him while he trailed his mouth across her cheeks and to her ear. He licked her earlobe as he clutched at her waist. Slowly, he slipped his hand up and under her shirt, touching her soft skin.

She gasped and wiggled under him. He groaned and returned his mouth to hers to kiss her deeply as he found her breast.

Bang. Thump.

Neil jumped at the sound, and his heart sped up when he heard whimpers coming from the guest room. Breathing heavy, he jumped up and rushed to the door. One hand on the handle and the other poised to knock, he called through the door. "Ms. Jacquie?"

No answer.

Chapter Nine

Hannah pulled her shirt down and sat up. She combed her fingers through her hair and pulled it back into the band Neil had tugged loose minutes before.

"Ms. Jacquie, you okay? You have ten seconds before I come in," Neil threatened.

Hannah moved toward him as he twisted the knob and opened the door. *He's going to go in and see another woman minutes after what we did on the couch?* Her stomach clenched. She should have known he'd be like this. Heat spread up her neck as she took a step toward her bag.

"I knocked my tea over going to the bathroom!" An older woman's voice called out.

Hannah spun around and rushed to the bedroom door, grabbing Neil's arm before he entered the empty room. When he glanced at her, she nodded toward the bathroom door along the far wall where it stood open a few inches. She lowered her voice before speaking, "Let me check on her." An elderly woman made her jealous? *Losing it fast, girlfriend.*

Neil tipped his head at the open door before walking over to pick up the tea cup lying on its side next to the bed.

Hannah skirted toward the bathroom door. Tapping lightly, she called, "Ma'am? My name is Hannah. I'm a friend of Neil's. Do you need any help?"

The woman chuckled. "Oh no, I'm good now. I could use your help getting back in bed in one minute, though."

Hannah waited until the woman was done and opened the door. Her eyes widened at the older woman standing before her. Her lips lifted as she assisted Ms. Jacquie back to bed.

Once tucked in, the woman touched Hannah's hand. "Thank you so much. You are a pretty thing. Neil hasn't mentioned you, and he never brings anyone home with him. This must be serious then?" She winked.

Hannah's heart skipped. "Um, I'm staying here for just tonight." She told the woman about the attempted break-in and resulting decision.

"Oh, you poor, dear girl." Hannah's spine tingled when the woman shifted her gaze toward the door behind her. "You, young man, need to triple check her door. Make sure it's safe. And she looks a bit peaked. Get her a cup of tea too."

"Yes, ma'am," Neil responded. "After I give you yours." He set a fresh cup of tea on the nightstand.

Hannah rose. "Good night, Ms. Jacquie. It was a pleasure to meet you."

"You, too, and I'll see you in the morning." Ms. Jacquie switched her gaze to Neil. "You are going to let her stay in your room, yes? You can sleep on that lumpy couch of yours."

"Of course," he said, then grinned. "The couch is closer to your bedroom too. That was my plan all along."

The woman laughed, and her face turned a slight shade of pink. "Oh, off with you."

Neil laughed as he and Hannah walked out of the room.

"I'm okay on the couch. It's not lumpy," Hannah whispered.

Neil shook his head. "You heard her. Besides, I won't be able to sleep in my room picturing you on that couch. You've got the master bath in there too."

Hannah's mouth dropped open as Neil's words sunk in. Her body hummed at the memory of what they'd just done on the couch. She clamped her lips together and nodded. Spinning away, she rushed to his room and closed the door on his low chuckle. *Drat him.* She took several breaths, stomped in the bathroom, and washed her face. A short time later, she crawled into the large bed covered in a bright quilt. Neil and quilts? *Odd.*

She rolled to her side, and Neil's scent instantly surrounded her. She pressed her face to his pillow and inhaled deeply. He'd treated Ms. Jacquie like family and cared for her. Maybe he wasn't so bad. Maybe he had a tough exterior but was soft on the inside? She sighed. Maybe she wanted to believe that. She frowned, punched the pillow, and closed her eyes. *Sleep.*

****

Neil woke to the aroma of bacon and biscuits the following morning. His stomach rumbled and urged him to hurry and fill it. He rubbed his face and opened his eyes to see Hannah moving around in his little apartment-sized kitchen. Ms. Jacquie sat at the small dinette table sipping coffee, with her leg propped on the chair across from her.

He rose and like a zombie on the scent of fresh food, beelined it to the coffee pot. After pouring a cup, he glanced around. Both women observed him in silence. His face heated before he cleared his throat.

"What?" Neil asked.

Hannah chuckled. "Nothing. After you wash up, breakfast will be served. I took the liberty of using what you had on hand, along with Ms. Jacquie's staples, and made homemade biscuits with bacon and scrambled eggs. I hope you don't mind."

"No, not at all. Sounds and smells great. Be right back," he said whipping around and aiming for the bathroom.

Once done, he joined them and sat down to eat. Full breakfast without having to pay a bill...and in my own home. *Nice.* He looked up to see Ms. Jacquie grinning. He tilted his head. She shook her head in response, and he frowned. *What's that about?*

Hannah sat down and started eating. A peaceful silence filled the room. His shoulders loosened, and his gut settled down. The hot food filled his stomach while he relaxed.

"I've got my cousin Anna coming by to take me to my eye doctor. We're doing lunch, so I won't be back until later this evening. Unless I decide to spend the night. I'll call and let you know later," Ms. Jacquie announced.

"I've got to get back to my apartment and call a locksmith," Hannah said.

"No," Neil spoke.

"No?"

"No. You don't need to call a locksmith. I can do it for free. We just need to stop at the hardware store and get a lock. I've got to get some for my house also." *Blast it. Those cameras and microphones better be gone too.*

"You don't need to do that for me. And what house?"

"I know I don't. But I'm going to do it anyway," he said, pushing away his empty plate.

"Why?" she asked.

"Because then I'll know it's done correctly."

She sat back and frowned at him. "You don't think I can find a competent locksmith? It is my apartment you know." She rose and took her empty plate to the sink. "I don't need a keeper," she said over her shoulder. "What house?"

The doorbell rang, keeping him from responding. He answered the door. A uniformed driver announced he was there on behalf of Ms. Jacquie's cousin and would be assisting her to the car.

Neil's brows rose. A driver? Just how loaded was that cousin of hers? He turned and before he could say anything, Ms. Jacquie tapped his arm.

"Help me with my coat. I'm ready to go," she said.

He helped her and closed the door after she left. When he returned to the kitchen, Hannah had the dishes cleared and stacked in the washer. He walked up behind her. There had to be a better way to get her to let him install the door locks. *Think.*

"I'm not questioning your competency." He stepped closer and whispered, "I wish you'd let me help."

She whipped around, and her eyes widened at his proximity. He leaned in slightly and focused on those lush lips of hers. The memory of their softness, her taste, filled him, and he hardened. Pulse racing, he glanced up, and found her gaze had dipped to his mouth. *Yes.* He lowered his head and brushed her lips with his. He licked her bottom lip, and she gasped.

Neil captured her mouth with a kiss. Wrapping his arms around Hannah, he pressed her against the counter and let the heat flood his body. Her curves beckoned him, and he stroked her back, then trailed down to her soft, rounded bottom. He squeezed, and she moaned in his mouth. He tilted his head and took the kiss deeper. Neil wanted her more than he'd ever wanted any woman. He savored her mouth, taking his breath from her, existing only for this moment. Yes, I know he and hers in the above, but couldn't come up with a way to change them.

His mind became lost in the feel of her, and his body screamed for more. More touching, more heat, more—Hannah. He rocked his hips against hers, and heat scored through his center when she whimpered. His lips skimmed her neck and trail down to a feminine shoulder. The woman was beautiful, and her porcelain skin sweet and salty to his tongue. He again trailed kisses along her throat, and to the area above her blouse—where the top of her breasts lay bare above the collar. His little chef gasped when he grabbed the back of her thighs and lifted her on top of the counter, wrapping her legs around his hips, with her hands clinging to his shirt as he pressed against the center of her heat.

"I want you," Neil whispered in her ear. Need rippled through him.

She stiffened and leaned back. She shook her head. "No, I'm sorry. No." She pushed him away and jumped down. "That shouldn't have happened. I'm sorry."

"Stop apologizing, woman," Neil spat and stepped

back. "I started it." His body berated him for stopping. His muscles tightened, and his mind fought with desire. "No is no in my book."

"I—" she whispered.

"Fine. It's fine," he said, his voice rough with desire. He ran his hand through his hair and stepped farther away. Space. He needed space. What were they talking about?

Hannah wrapped her arms around herself and looked down. A blush stole up her neck and infused a pretty pink in her cheeks. Why was she embarrassed? Damn, he had to say something, or he would kiss her again.

He cleared his throat. "So, I'll change the locks for you. I'll come by this afternoon and do it."

"What house?" she asked.

"Huh?"

"You said you needed to get locks for your house. You live here, so what house?"

"Oh." He sighed. "I recently inherited a house. It needs work. But first, I need to change the locks. So, I'll change yours too." *And maybe he'd get another kiss.*

"Fine. Whatever," she said picking at her shirt then continued, "You go on ahead. I'm going to grab a shower first, then head out."

"Why?" Neil asked. Did she want to get away from him that bad?

"Because I have errands to run. It'll be fine," she wiped off the counter before she pulled out her phone. She shooed him with a wave. "Go on. I'll see you later."

Neil's jaw tightened. He stormed to his bedroom,

jerked a suitcase out of his closet and tossed in clothes, towels, and whatever else his hands landed on. He slammed it shut, zipped it closed, and returned to the kitchen. Hannah's back faced him while she spoke on the phone ordering a cab. He grunted, then blew out a breath, and left. *Stubborn woman.*

****

Neil checked the clock when he arrived at Hanson House. Hanson House. It was his house now. Garrett House? He blew out a breath, snagged the groceries he'd bought on the way over, along with his suitcase, and headed in. The aroma of baked oatmeal cookies assaulted him the second he stepped inside. He slumped his normally upright frame. So not fair. How had she figured out his favorite cookie? Could ghosts read minds?

He put away the groceries and placed his suitcase in the bedroom before returning outside. He found the shipping pallet with the items he'd ordered near the storage shed. He rubbed his hands together and grinned. After making his way to the plastic wrapped boxes, he scanned the sky. A few clouds buffeted their way slowly toward the east. No wind blew to stir up the heavy morning air. He tugged his gloves out of his back pocket along with a box cutter and worked on removing the plastic.

Neil inspected the first box containing the cabinet doors finding no scratches or damage on the exterior. One by one, he carried eight boxes, that contained two cabinet doors each, inside and set them on the dining room floor next to the sink he'd removed earlier in the week. He returned to the pallet and smoothed a hand along the long pieces of granite bound in bubble wrap under plastic. Bending at the knees, he grunted and lifted the heavy piece.

Carefully, he made his way back inside and leaned it up against the wall. He made three more trips with smaller pieces of granite. After placing them on the floor, Neil peeled off his coat and gloves to run his hands along the cabinets he'd finished sanding and staining after removing the sink. *Nice and dry.* For the next hour, Neil installed the cabinet doors with their shiny hinges while listening to a small radio he'd found in a closet.

"Must you make so much racket?" Muriel's voice rang out. "I declare a woman cannot be expected to sustain this amount of noise for such long periods of time."

Neil ignored the voice, grabbed the blade tool, and cut along the caulking line of the countertop. The radio buzzed, crackled, then fell silent. He paused, grimacing at the old thing.

"There, now I can have some peace to think."

Neil shrugged, grabbed the hammer, and began banging under the countertop, lifting it slightly. He worked slowly around the edge until he got it loosened. Using the edge of the hammer, he leveraged the long piece of laminate up.

"Argh!" she screamed. The sound echoed off the walls then faded.

Good. Neil pried off the countertop. It broke and cracked in several areas. He chuckled. Demolition time. Within minutes, he had several chunks of the old laminate counter on the floor and using the hammer worked on removing the rest. Once done, he carried the debris out and tossed it off to the side of the yard. The dumpster he'd ordered would arrive this weekend.

Returning to the kitchen, he got a bottle of water and drank deep gulps. Grabbing the sandpaper, he sanded off the remaining caulk and glue until it was all gone. He installed the large pieces of plywood he'd cut on top of the lower cabinets and nailed them down. Neil stepped back and surveyed the work completed so far. Good. He picked up the small radio and jiggled it, turning the power button off then on again. Static met him while he spun the dial searching for another station to listen to.

When bagpipes blared a bouncing song, he laughed and set the radio back on the counter, cranking the volume higher. Take that. He twisted around, grabbed the epoxy gun, and squeezed a trail of the adhering agent all along the top of the plywood. Setting the tube aside, he slipped on his gloves and blew out a breath before heaving the large piece of granite over to the sink portion of the counterspace and set it down. He pushed and shoved it in place and then stood back, grinning. "Do I know how to measure or what?" Neil called out to no one, then rubbed his hands together. He repeated the process until the remaining pieces were all set in place.

He grabbed the epoxy again, along with a putty knife, and slipped a bead of epoxy between the granite pieces at the seams. With his work rag Neil wiped away the excess glue, then attached and adjusted clamps over soft foam. That'd take fifteen minutes to set with the clamps holding everything in place. He spun around, opened the fridge, and picked out a sandwich. Ripping off the wrapper, Neil bit into the cold ham and cheese. He chewed while he gathered the remaining plastic and wrapping, then carried them outside to dump with the rest of the trash.

When he returned, he leaned against the wall, and examined his work while he ate. The gray and black granite complemented the stainless-steel appliances. Neil glanced at the clock. Enough time to take a shower, dress, and lock up before hitting the road for his meeting with Cast and the school's dean.

He shot a last look at the granite reflecting sunshine from the windows before heading upstairs. His chest tightened at the image of Hannah standing and mixing ingredients on the newly installed countertops. *I bet she'd love this.*

"I declare, you've done a very nice job here. Even though all that clamor would have given anyone a horrendous headache. I do so hope you plan to repaint this room as well. Those white walls are dreadfully drab."

Neil frowned and shot for the stairs.

"It's quite rude to run off during a conversation. I could simply follow you, you know."

Oh hell no. Imagination or not, that was not going to happen. He paused on the first step and filled his lungs with air before pushing it back out. His mouth split into a wide grin.

"Well, come on up then and watch the show," he declared and ignoring the gasp behind him, rushed up the stairs.

Chapter Ten

Neil arrived at Hannah's school near two, and the parking lot's activity confirmed class changes in progress. Whoever or whatever Muriel was, she'd almost pushed him to his limits threatening to follow him upstairs. The scene flashed back in his mind, and he smirked. She was quick to leave when he told her he was about to get in the shower, and if she wanted to watch he didn't mind. He blew out a breath. *Focus.* He needed to focus now.

Students dressed in chef jackets grouped together discussing recipes and class events buzzed in the background, as he made his way to the administrative offices. Dean Hampton had agreed to meet and discuss the current state of the competition, and only through a little pressure on his part, did the man finally admit to there being an issue.

Competitors being knocked out of the competition wasn't such an issue, but the threat of bad publicity worked on this man. He nodded at Cast who sat in the interior waiting room and grunted when he took the seat next to him.

"I've been here thirty minutes, dude. What's up?" Cast asked.

"Had to stop and fix Hannah's locks."

Cast shook his head. "Gotta be careful there, partner. Besides, it's not like she's your type, true?"

"Type? I have a type?" Neil asked in a low voice. He rolled his shoulders to loosen the tightness in them.

Cast lifted his hands. "Your women tend to be on the thin side. That Hannah has some set of curves."

Neil scowled and twisted to glare. "And there's something wrong with having curves?" He faced forward and muttered, "Don't answer that. I know what your type is, too, buddy, and one day, maybe you'll realize it's not all in the body shape."

His friend leaned in. "Hey, watch the tone. It's not bad, a surprise, is all. Besides, the bad idea is getting involved with her."

Neil grunted again, shifting his gaze to the woman approaching them.

"Mr. Hampton is ready to see you," the receptionist announced.

Neil and Cast rose and strode into the office. Dean Hampton got to his feet from behind his desk and shook their hands before settling back.

"Officer Garrett, I've reviewed the information you forwarded to me. I agree there is a situation here."

Neil leaned forward. "A situation?"

The dean raised his hand, palm forward. "I'm sorry. I don't mean to minimize the issues involved here. I agree with your findings and will support you fully in your investigation. However, my concern is that you believe one of the students is a killer. That these events—that I believed to be accidents—are not accidents at all. We can't have that here. I'm in charge of the safety for all students when they are on this campus. If I must, I'll close the campus…not that I want to do that at all, if possible."

Neil shook his head. "That's not needed, nor will it

help in any way. In fact, what I'm proposing will only work if the school is still in session."

"And you are positive that just the competitors are at risk?"

Cast nodded. "We believe someone is trying to sway the competition. Our investigation points to another student. However, that's not to say it couldn't be someone else."

"Such as?" the dean asked.

"We don't know yet. That's why we're here. The alleged accidents are happening only when the competitors are together." Neil glanced at Cast. At his partner's nod, he continued, "This is what we'd like to do."

They spent the next two hours with the dean outlining their plan to catch the killer in the act. The dean called in the campus security chief, and the four of them negotiated the details of how they would have Cast slip in undercover as a local magazine reporter looking to do a write-up on the competition. They'd have cameras hidden in and around the kitchen area and security, along with back-up officers who would cover the exterior doors.

Once every detail had been discussed and noted, the meeting ended.

Neil and Cast stopped by Neil's car afterward.

"You think this will work?" Cast asked.

"I hope so. Otherwise, he sounded like he'd be ready to cancel the competition. If he does, Hannah will never speak to me again." Neil's stomach clenched.

"You've never been one to walk outside the line, dude," Cast remarked. "You sure you're not too close to this?"

Neil rolled his shoulders and frowned. "No. Maybe. No. I've got it under control."

"Yeah, sounds like you're absolutely positive about that." Cast snickered and smacked Neil's shoulder.

"Go to hell," Neil responded.

"Dude, I intend to be driving the bus there," Cast retorted, then laughed as he spun around and sauntered away.

He shook his head as his partner drove off, then got in his car and cranked the engine. Sitting there, he recalled Hannah's last words and the sorrow in her voice. His stomach burned, and he rubbed his nape. *Damn.* He had it bad. He whipped open his case book and read his notes again. He hadn't missed anything. Cast had double-checked, and if something was missing, he'd notice. He checked the clock. He had hours before Ms. Jacquie would be returning to the apartment. Time to get some grunt work done.

An hour later, Neil pulled back into the Hanson House drive and cut the engine. He tipped his head back and to the sides stretching his neck muscles before getting out of the car. The late afternoon heat combined with the showers due tonight rocketed the humidity level to high. He took off his shirt, grabbed the new lock-sets he'd purchased and tossed them toward the front door. Spinning around, he strode to the storage shed. Upon opening the doors, he found nothing had been disturbed. Safe neighborhood.

Neil grabbed the circular saw, square ruler, pencil, and measuring tape. He headed back to the front porch and set the items to the left of the door near the stack of lumber. Lifting the tarp, he pulled out eight boards and checked them for any warping. Once done, he measured the length of the porch deck he planned to replace and began cutting the boards to fit. At least with the new support beams, this project would be done in no time. He paused and unlocking the front door, slipped inside, while the cool air swept across his skin. After grabbing a bottle of water, he returned outside, twisted the top, and slugged down a large amount of the cool liquid.

He wiped his brow with his forearm and drank more water. Stepping off the porch, Neil moved ten feet away before turning to study the area he'd planned to work on. He dipped his chin, returned, and pulled off the first piece of plywood—sliding it off the porch, then dropping it near the stack of wood. He grunted when the next board refused to budge. It'd been nailed in place. D'uh. He strode to the shed, located a hammer and nails, and returned.

Dark musical notes along with the vibration in his pocket made him drop the tools and dig out his cell phone.

"Garrett," he answered.

"It's Marcus, I need a favor."

Neil straightened. Why was Hannah's brother calling?

"What's wrong?" What would it be like to get phone calls that didn't equate to a problem?

"My landlord...landlady's investors have had problems staying alive. The latest is missing in action. It's gonna cripple her...Victoria's business start-up. The local cops are saying coincidence. I don't agree."

Neil swiped a palm over his forehead. No way could he leave Hannah right now. "Okay, so you need to confirm it's not a coincidence before pushing the locals.?"

"Yes, that's all I need."

"I've got a friend who's a private investigator working out of downtown Newnan. I'll text you his number. Tell him I referred you, and he should be able to help."

Silence.

"Marcus, you got that?"

"Um, yeah."

Hairs stiffened on the back of his neck. Neil frowned. "What?"

"Victoria's business is akin to ghost hunting. Your guy gonna have a problem with that?"

"No, he's into shit like that, I think." Something like that. Neil glanced at the hammer and nails lying on the ground. "I'm not sure exactly what he's into, but he's cool."

"Okay, thanks."

Neil disconnected the call, sent the text with Jordan's name, then rolled his shoulders. Dude's got problems bigger than his leg. He let the image of Hannah and their morning discussion seep into his mind while he worked the nails loose on the remaining plywood—pulling them out, then stacking them on top of the first one he'd dropped. His heart pounded at the idea of the fiery woman getting hurt in any way. He mentally ran through the checklist of their plan to catch the killer while he measured, then set each cut board in place, nailing them to the support beams. He couldn't find any holes in their plans.

Neil's phone shrilled again. Once again, he dug it out. Ms. Jacquie. Hm. He answered.

"Honey, I'm not coming back tonight and wanted to let you know. I'll call you early tomorrow."

"Everything okay? He asked, ignoring the sweat dripping off of him.

"Oh, yes, dear. Just a change of plans."

They said their farewells, and he repocketed his phone. When he sat, and secured the last board, he bounded off the porch and examined his work. The long boards of the porch deck made it safer to walk on. Once painted, it'd be a nice place to set chairs to monitor the neighborhood. Or a swing would work. He pictured Hannah sitting on a front porch swing with the wind tossing those gorgeous curls of hers while she rocked.

A ripple of electricity shot through his body. Stomping toward the plywood boards he'd removed, he lifted and carried each one around the back of the house to place inside the greenhouse for storage. After the last piece had been placed, he stopped and surveyed the room. He scrutinized every inch of the ceiling and still found no openings that would allow water to enter. He inspected the brick-built pony walls topped by metal framing and more plexiglass. No breaks. Hmm.

Neil wiped off dirt from his pant legs, then paused when a small hum broke the silence. He stilled, holding his breath while the hum increased in volume then turned into a hiss. He blew out his breath and scanned the room. What was that? Suddenly a pop poked through the silence and water sprayed down from the small plastic pipes hanging from the ceiling.

Neil ducked, covered his head with his arms, and ran out laughing. *Well, hell.* Of course, the greenhouse would have a watering system for the plants. He shook his head and body like a dog after a bath, spraying water in every direction. He strode around the house and pushed open the front door. A hard-cold wind whipped at him, chilling his wet skin. He sucked in a quick breath and stepped over the threshold.

"I hope you intend to take off those muddy boots before you come any farther inside this house."

Neil planted his feet on the black plastic bag still sitting on the floor in the entry. His gaze combed the kitchen. No white mist or cloud. Damn if he was going to be taking orders from…anyone. It's time the lady understood who owned this house now.

Chapter Eleven

The group of students exiting the school Friday night, congregated in small clusters, whispering short quick words, that caused an incessant buzzing in Hannah's ears. She walked alone, staring at the pavement, ignoring anyone who attempted to include her in a conversation. Her tears fell, and she gasped for air, trying to ease the tightness in her chest. She ran her palm over her lower belly in an attempt to push back the rolling bile threatening to erupt.

Chuck Anderson had recently turned eighteen. The youngest of the competitors had been admitted to the hospital. His family advised the school he'd been suffering from arsenic poisoning. *Arsenic.*

She grabbed for her car keys when they slipped through her fingers dropping on the dark asphalt at her feet. She bent over, and her head swam. She dropped to her knees, clasping her keys close within her clenched hands. The keyring bit into her palm sending pain up her arm. *This can't be happening. It can't.*

Her phone rang, and she jerked, falling off balance, and landing on her bottom. She almost didn't answer. She almost let it just ring and ring. Almost. The image of Rose flitted in her mind, and she quickly tapped her phone.

"Hello, Rose," she whispered.

The same conversation each night ensued. After

the call, Hannah stood, unlocked her car, and got in. She glanced around and noted most everyone had left. A dark blue sedan sat four spots behind her with its engine running. Likely another student calling home to let their parents know what happened and update them on the closing of the school.

Closed. For how long?

Hannah put her car in gear and drove away. After leaving the school parking lot, her engine started making a strange clicking sound. She frowned as she stopped at the red light. The noise grew louder when she turned the vehicle. Her heart raced when she looked in the rearview mirror and found the blue sedan behind her.

Probably a coincidence she thought, but then engine breathed a puff of smoke. *What on earth?* Turning on her emergency flashers, she steered the car to the curb. Hannah grabbed the owner's manual and searched her dashboard for indicator lights. Nothing. *Weird.* She held her breath as the blue sedan cruised slowly past. As it turned onto another road, she let out a sigh and flipped through the book again before tossing it in the back. A mechanic she was not. Who was she kidding?

She counted to ten, and then twisted the key to see if the car would start again. With her window cracked, she frowned when a clicking echoed inside her car. *Shoot.* She slumped back in her seat. The back road was empty like she preferred. No traffic to keep her from getting home at a decent hour. *Think.* She couldn't call the car service because she'd let that lapse. Marcus lived too far away. Mom and Dad lived too far away. *Drat. Taxi, then.*

Hannah gasped as the blue sedan drove up the road from behind her, and her pulse picked up. *Okay, stay calm.* That's not another student. Why had they driven in a circle? She checked and relocked her doors and then punched in Neil's number.

"Hannah? What's wrong?" Neil asked.

"How do you know something's wrong? Never mind. My car died, and there's a blue sedan who is circling around. I think they were following me."

"Where are you? Lock your doors and stay on the phone with me," Neil ordered. "If they stop, hang up, and dial 9-1-1."

"Okay. I'm on Evans Road. It leads directly behind the school property. Coming out of the lot, you turn right at the light. And my doors are already locked."

"Good girl. I'm on my way."

Hannah shivered when the blue sedan passed her and turned left again at the same street as before. "They passed by again. That's twice now."

"As long as they don't stop, we're good," Neil assured her. "I'm nearly an hour away. But, I'll be there in thirty minutes."

"Okay. Okay." Her heart threatened to burst out of her chest. "Wait, why? Aren't you home?" Newnan wasn't an hour away. "Calling the police would be faster, don't you think?"

"Ms. Jacquie decided to stay with her cousin, and I'm working out of my house in Senoia. You want to call the police on a suspicious car? Call them if they stop. Otherwise, keep talking to me."

"Why?" She gripped the steering wheel.

"Talk to me, honey, so I can be sure you're okay. What's the latest at the school? You're out early."

Hannah relayed the events of earlier, the news about Chuck, and the school's closure.

"Closed for how long?"

"I don't know. It's Friday, so at least for the weekend. Maybe Monday too. I won't know until I check my student site." Her hands shook as she pressed the phone closer to her ear.

His voice soothed her nerves, easing the tightness in her chest, and she breathed easier. She kept scanning the road in front of her and rechecked her rearview mirror.

"Hannah? Honey?"

Neil's voice pierced her surveillance.

"Don't call me honey." Damn, the man got on her nerves, even while keeping her from freaking out.

"I'm fifteen minutes out. Hold on."

"I am. I'm fine. How fast are you going?" Where the heck did he think she'd go? No way on Earth did she consider jumping out and running. Stupid, she was not.

"Don't worry about that. Let me know if you spot them again. Now, keep talking to me," he ordered.

Why did he always order her around? A few minutes, that seemed like hours, passed before a set of headlights blinded her from behind. Her throat tightened, and she gasped for air.

"There's headlights behind me. It might be them," Hannah whispered. She scooted down in the seat, her heart pounding.

"No, it's me, honey. It's me. I'm sorry, I should have told you. I'm going to flash the lights so you know, okay?"

Neil flashed the lights, and Hannah's breath

whooshed out.

"Okay, okay." She released her death grip on the steering wheel and disconnected the call.

Before she could unlock the door, Neil loomed on the other side of her driver's window and knocked. She unlocked the door and squeezed out in the small space he'd allowed. "Want to give me some space?"

He grabbed her arm and pulled her along with him. "Keep moving," he ordered...again. He opened the passenger side of his car, and pushing her head down, practically shoved her in his car like she'd seen police do in the movies. He was too strong to fight. Neil then slammed her door shut, and a beep confirmed he'd locked her in.

What was with this guy? She punched the unlock button, only to have it click back. She glared at Neil through the window. He shook his head, pivoted, and stomped back to her car.

She crossed her arms and waited. *Neanderthal.*

Yet, she breathed easier and her body relaxed slightly. Neil walked around her car and up the road about twenty feet before returning. He grabbed her belongings from her car and returned, tossing them in the back seat behind her, then locked her back in. She frowned when he wrote a note, tucked it in her windshield, locked her car, and returned to her. They were leaving her car here?

When he got in beside her, she twisted and faced him. "We can't just leave it here."

"We can and we are. I'll arrange to pick it up tomorrow."

"There's nothing wrong with it, other than a clicking sound. So, why can't you fix it and simply follow me home?"

"Because"—he cranked on the engine—"whoever is following you likely knows where you live as well. You're coming home with me."

Hannah swallowed and inhaled a deep breath. *Calm.* "No, I'm not."

"Yes, you are."

"I am not staying at your apartment tonight." No way. Without Ms. Jacquie there, they'd be alone. Flashes of her last time there and their tussle on the couch danced around Hannah's mind. Her body heated. It'd be too tempting. *He* was too tempting.

"What?" she asked when she realized Neil had said something.

"We're not going to my apartment. We're going to the house I'm renovating. There's plenty of rooms to pick from. No couch."

"Why?"

"We're not taking the chance that they intended to scare you first before jumping you at your place. It'll be safer at the house."

Fine. She was going with him. More rooms meant more space, right? Her body tingled. Who was she kidding?

"Why the house and not your apartment, then?" she said.

"Because no one has seen you go there. I don't know how long you've been followed, and if whoever followed you tonight has followed you before, they'll know my place too."

"But you'll be there. Certainly, they can't be so stupid as to follow me to a cop's house."

Neil grunted. "There's no way we can know if

they're aware of my occupation, honey."

Hannah shivered. "Fine."

****

A short time later, Hannah's jaw slacked when Neil pulled into a gravel drive, the tires crunching, while fog, caused by a mid-fall temperature drop, floated on the ground. The interior of the car kept her toasty, along with illicit images of Neil. They'd driven in silence most of the way, which worked for her.

"It's in pretty bad shape," Hannah commented, noting the condition of the porch roof. It looked like it'd fall down around them. "You sure it's safe to stay here?"

"I know the outside looks pretty rough. But it's solid. I've checked it. It'll look that way until the weather warms up and I can work longer hours outside. In the meantime, I'm working on the interior."

Hannah smirked while reaching for her bags. "You checked it? You doing building inspections on the side?"

"No. I know a little about houses, so I know what to look for."

Interesting. When had he found time to work on houses with the kind of job he had? Her brother, Sam, told her homicide detectives had long hours and rarely did anything other than their jobs…and maybe party.

"Who is doing the inside work?"

"Me," he said sharply.

She raised her palm before continuing, "Okay. I didn't realize you do this kind of thing." *Touchy subject.*

He unlocked the doors, and she got out, bracing for the cold blast of air. She jerked open the back door,

131

grabbed the rest of her things, spun around, then stopped short. Neil stood directly behind her.

She gasped. "What?" Why did he always do that?

He took her things and headed around the back of the house. "Follow me. I installed the front deck earlier, but there's no porch light. Without rails, I wouldn't want you to accidently step off the side."

She dipped her chin and followed him carefully over the brittle grass to a set of glass doors. While he unlocked them, she peered inside.

"At least you left a light on." From her position, she took in the dimly lit side room. Hardwood floors and plain walls. It looked bigger on the inside, and her heart tripped with the sudden warmth that flooded her. She frowned. She only had that kind of warmth while home.

The click of the lock echoed against the night, and she shifted her gaze back to Neil, who appeared to be glued in place on the small porch. He stared inside the house.

"What's wrong?"

Neil shook his head. "Nothing. I just remembered something for work."

No, he didn't. The hairs on the back of her neck tickled. She studied Neil while he pulled open the doors and stepped slowly inside. He paused, then stepped back out, waving at her to precede him. She walked lightly over the threshold and paused to stomp her shoes on the rope rug resting inside the door.

"May I look around?" Hannah asked.

"Sure," Neil said.

She toed off her wet shoes and in stocking feet padded through the large living area scanning the bare walls. Her gaze caught on the large fireplace to her right, and she moved closer—running her fingertips along the mantle. Her lips lifted when a picture of Christmas stockings hanging on this one flashed in her mind. She pressed her lips together and spun around.

With her first step into the dining area, she twisted back and forth, staring slack-jawed at the kitchen. For a moment, her vision wavered. The kitchen, in the process of being remodeled sported a stainless-steel double sink sitting under a wide double window darkened by the night. The cabinets with etched glass on the front hugged a double pastry oven and a gas stove top. To the left, a commercial-sized refrigerator with ice and water dispensers met her gaze. Her breath caught on the vision of her dream kitchen.

A hand on her lower back made her jerk and blink. A large picnic basket sat atop granite countertops that spanned the kitchen. She bit her lip. How had he known? Her heart sank at the reality that this was not her kitchen.

"You okay?" Neil's deep voice murmured behind her.

"Yes," she responded in a low voice. Her stomach growled when the aroma of baking cookies assaulted her. She peered at the oven. It was off. She scanned the counters, but no cooking trays or cooling racks were present. *Weird.* "You cook?"

"No," he said gruffly and tugged her arm. "Come on. I'll show you where you can crash for the night. I got a second air mattress the other day as a back-up until my furniture arrives."

She pulled back from him. "Wait a minute. I smell cookies. If you don't cook"—she waved her arm toward the kitchen—"then who does? You've got a double convection oven installed here. And where are the cookies? I could use a snack." She smiled.

"What cookies? Is that why there's two ovens? I don't smell any cookies. I don't know what you're talking about," Neil retorted and then frowned toward the kitchen before walking away. "Come on. It's getting late and I'm whipped. You must be imagining things."

She placed her fists on her hips and sniffed. *Yep, that's cookies*. Anyone could smell and know what it was. She peered inside the refrigerator. Her shoulders slumped. No cookies. Beer, milk, orange juice, eggs, and sausage. No fruit, vegetables, nor basic staples. She bent lower and studied the package on the bottom shelf. It looked like week-old pepperoni pizza. She shuddered. *Ugh.* She shut the door and glanced around. In the far corner sat an old 1950s bread box.

Neil's footsteps pounded directly above her. He must've gone upstairs. He could wait.

She walked over and lifted the lid. Empty. *Drat.* How could Neil be so mean as to make cookies and lie about it? He needed to understand that in order for her to trust him, he'd have to return the favor. Even with something as small as cookies. Her stomach growled. Especially cookies. She closed the box and padded off to find him.

She located the stairs, grasped the banister, and stepped on the first stair. A woman laughed softly from around the corner, and Hannah paused. She searched the bottom floor, inspecting each of the spacious rooms. She frowned when she arrived at the stairs again. No woman…and no cookies.

Hannah climbed the stairs and paused at the

landing. The whooshing of an air pump echoed from the hall to her left along with Neil's grumbling. *Not yet.* She turned, skimming her fingers along the top of the aged banister. She paused and peered down at the living area below. The sparse room with hardwood floors remained quiet. She pushed open the door to her left and gasped. Inside were floor-to-ceiling bookcases on either side of the room. While one side stood empty and dusty, the opposite unit practically overflowed with books. An oversized bay window allowed pale moonlight to shine in and dance with the dust covered antique desk.

Stepping closer to the filled bookcase, she studied the spines of the collection. Various sized books advertised ancient maps, historical references, and law books. She bent over and bit her lip to keep from laughing. The two bottom shelves were completely packed with romance novels. Reaching for the sliding ladder, she pulled it to her, placed one foot on the bottom rung, and stepped up, testing its sturdiness. *Okay, it's solid.* She carefully climbed until she could clearly read the titles of the top three shelves. Cookbooks. There had to be over a hundred of them. Her heart beat faster, and she grinned. She had to get a closer peek at these.

The sounds of the pump stopped, and she paused. Maybe in the morning. She descended the ladder and headed down the hall where Neil had been working. She found him in the last bedroom at the end of the hall. Her pulse picked up while he made up the extra-large air mattress. His large hands deftly fitted the sheets, covered the pillows, and laid two quilts atop the flat sheet.

The bed sat in the middle of the large room. This guest bedroom was huge. To her right was a doorway to a medium-sized vanity room. This room also contained a large bay window like the library. Brief pictures of how she'd decorate it—if it were hers—flitted into her mind. Suddenly, a vision of her and Neil in his apartment bed, appeared in her fantasy, and her body instantly reacted.

Neil stilled and spun around to face her. Heat spread up her neck and across her cheeks. She looked away and cleared her throat. *No.* He couldn't have known. She coughed.

"This is where I sleep?" she asked.

"Yeah."

"You?" Her heart skipped a beat.

He walked toward her and paused within a foot of her trembling body. His voice dropped low, "I can sleep here…if you want."

She blinked. "Where is your bed?" He studied her for a moment, then waved behind her. "Two doors down."

She nodded. "I assume all the facilities are okay to use?" *Just babble on.*

Neil grinned. "Of course."

Hannah took a step back. His male scent tugged at her along with the memories of their last kissing session.

"If you need anything, holler." He nodded then stepped around her.

She grabbed his arm. "Thank you."

He stared at her hand on his arm. She released him, and he smiled.

"You're welcome."

Then, before she could react, he grabbed her and pulled her to him. His mouth descended slowly as if to give her time to pull away. *No, not this time.* She met his mouth and tasted him. She struggled to wrap her arms around him, but he kept her in place. His mouth, hot and powerful, worked its magic on hers. Her eyes closed, and her body sang as warmth wrapped around her.

Suddenly, cold air met her face. She blinked and turned in time to see him head toward the door.

"Good night," he said.

Then he was gone. Her body shivered, and she bit her lip to keep from whimpering and calling him back. *Drat it.* It was obvious he wanted her. She wanted him too. It was unlikely any kind of relationship between them would last. Neanderthals and chefs did not mix well. No, wait. Neanderthals and she did not mix well. But…after all that had happened. What if she was next on the 'hit list?' Did she want to go without experiencing what Neil could offer her? Was that shallow of her? Did she care?

Her jaw clenched. *Jeesh. Just make a decision.* A low moan echoed behind her. She spun around. Nothing there. The wind whipped a branch slamming it against the window. Hannah shuddered. The creepy moan came again with a small scratching sound that crawled on her skin. She shuddered again. Too much. She'd had too much to deal with tonight. That's what was wrong. Her nerves were at their breaking point. She took a step toward the door, but all the lights blacked out. She squeaked and ran out of the room.

Chapter Twelve

Neil paused before climbing in bed when the entire house went dark. *What the hell?* He held his breath, listening for any odd noises. Hannah's squeak and rushing steps reached him. *Hannah.*

He rushed into the hall.

"Neil?" Hannah whispered.

His eyes adjusted to the darkness, and she stood there locked in place. He moved toward her, then stopped several inches away. The white of her eyes shone, and she trembled.

"It's okay, honey. The power's gone out. I'll go check the fuse box," Neil assured her with a quick squeeze to her arm.

"No, it's not that. I heard a moaning before the lights went out. Didn't you hear it?"

"No, I didn't hear anything. Likely the wind outside is picking up a bit. We're supposed to have rain tonight. I haven't had time to trim the tree branches."

She shook her head, and her body swayed. He stepped forward, and she wove her arms around his shoulders. He curled his arms around her soft curves and pulled her close, lowering his head to speak into her ear. "I've got you." And he did too. He held her, and he always would, if she'd let him. He sucked in a quick breath at having his hands on her once more.

Hannah's shaking eased, and she mumbled against

his chest. His body hardened at the contact. Her lavender scent wafted around and wrapped him in its cocoon. He inhaled and pulled her closer. *Wait.* She'd said something. Her chest vibrated against his, then she tipped her head away. He dipped his head lower to hear.

"I'm scared," she said in a low, trembling voice.

Hannah's next inhalation pressed her soft breasts against him. He bit his lip to stop from groaning and locked his knees. What the heck was she doing to him? His mind jumbled thoughts together when their bodies touched, and now…holding her, he was at her mercy.

"Neil," she whispered.

"I'm here," he responded. He tightened his hold trying to comfort her, yet much more of this and he'd carry her straight to his bed.

"I don't want to be alone."

Keep her calm. He could do that. *Wait…what?* Her words pierced his muddled thoughts. His body jerked, and desire burned through him. *Damn it all to hell.* She needed comfort, not sex. He tilted his head back to gaze into her eyes.

She wet her lips. "Will you stay with me?"

"I'm not sure if that's a good idea, sweetheart." *Crap.*

"Please."

Damn. That one word slayed him. Flayed him open and sliced at his tenuous hold against the fire threatening to consume him. *Ah, hell.* The heater fan kicked on, and he frowned. Power but no lights? Hannah wiggled against him. He swallowed, pushing his desire down deep and slammed a lock on it. Then he nodded. She shifted in his embrace, as he led her back to her room. Once inside, he searched for something…anything to focus on, instead of her.

"Get in, and I'll sleep on top of the covers," he whispered, searching the floor. *Don't look.*

Neil spotted a scratch on the floor. That's not too deep and a small amount of wood filler could hide it. The rustling of her getting into bed and settling down evaporated his next thought. He looked, and his heart raced as she drew herself beneath the covers, her hair splayed across the pillow. His every fantasy included that image. Then her gaze met his own. *Damn. Damn. Damn.*

He stretched out beside Hannah, leaving space between them. She shifted and laid her head on his chest. He wrapped his arm around her as she snuggled in closer, the heat of her body pressing against his side. Her other arm draped across his belly, and her palm pressed against his other side. He couldn't stop his left hand from reaching around and rubbing her wrist. Her skin, soft as melted chocolate intoxicated his senses.

Neil forced his body to relax and paced his breathing, as she shifted again, pulling the covers off her legs. He stifled a groan, blocking out the sexual images flooding in. He flexed his toes. *Focus on the toes…then the ankles…relax. Breathe.* One of her legs lifted and crossed over his. He stared at the ceiling. *Breathe, blast it.*

Her leg moved, and her thigh caressed his, drawing heat to his groin. He hardened painfully. *What the hell?* He lifted his head.

"Hannah?" he croaked out.

She raised her head and stretched up to place her lips on his. He stilled. She tilted her head, licked his bottom lip, then nipped it.

"Sweetheart…you've just been terrified. I don't think we should do this." His body flamed to life as she ignored him and continued licking, then nipping his lips. Need flicked along his nerves, his body shuddering. "Hannah, please," he begged. He couldn't resist her much longer.

"I want you," she whispered across his mouth.

Hunger flashed within him like a lit match to oil. The flame took over, and he rolled her onto her back, shoved away the remaining blankets and covered her with his body, bracing on his elbows. He showered kisses around her lips and along her jaw like a feather brushing her skin. He knew he should halt things at once, but damned if he could. Neil moved his mouth over hers, exploring its petal softness, then slipped his tongue inside to taste her sweetness. He shifted his weight and wove a hand in her silky hair, caressing the curls and the back of her neck, holding her still while he increased the pressure of his mouth. *He'd never tasted anything as sweet or felt anything as soft as this woman.* He trailed his palm over her shoulders, and down her side to her hips. Neil massaged her bottom, pulling her closer. *His need to make her his gnawed at him. His need to please her, to give equally, overcame his own need. Neil forced himself to go slow, to enjoy…to memorize everything.* His fingers slipped under her long T-shirt, and he smoothed his fingertips across her warm bare skin. A groan escaped his lips as he continued kissing her.

Hannah kissed him back with the same fervor he gave her, their tongues battling each other for taste and touch. His palm grazed her back, and she gasped. He trailed more kisses along her cheek to her chin and down her neck. She arched her back when he cupped her breast and lightly pinched her nipple. His mind filled with visions of Hannah laughing, arguing, lying on the bed, and his lungs filled with her scent, his soul filled with her warmth. *Salvation. She was his salvation.*

Neil tugged her head back and nipped on her neck. Her continued moans sent fire through him. He shook with the effort to slow down, failing miserably. She'd weakened every part of him. He met her gaze as he slowly lifted her shirt over her head, pinning her arms, then swooped down and closed his lips around the tight rosy bud of her breast. She gasped and arched into him while he lavished her taut nipple with his tongue. Neil ran his palms over her hips, pushing her panties down her smooth thighs. She lifted to help their descent while he switched to her other breast, flicking the nipple with his tongue.

Hannah's hands, delved into his hair, tugging and pulling. The sharp pinpricks across his scalp sent chills the length of his body. He rained kisses down her belly to the apex of her thighs. Neil inhaled deeply. *So sweet...so hot.*

His heart pounded against his chest, and his hands trembled as he opened her, placing his mouth against her. He groaned at the taste of her. When he stroked her petal-soft flesh with his tongue, Hannah bucked against him, her hands gripping the back of his head and pulling him in closer as her moans echoed into the darkness. *Mine.*

Enough. Neil wrenched up to his knees and wrestled with his jeans. She rose and tore at his zipper, both their hands working feverishly to release him. He grunted when his hips escaped, and her hand wrapped around his erection. He slung his head back as she stroked him with her slender warm fingers. His sucked in air as she fondled him. A ripple racked his body. *Mine. Nope. Hers. She owned him.*

A deep moan escaped his lips as her fingers wrapped around and tightened. His hips flexed involuntarily. *Blast it.* He placed his hand to hers, urging her to let go. If she kept on, he'd never make it inside her.

Neil pushed his pants and boxers down to his knees, then off, though she never released him. Instead, she pushed him back to the bed and took him in her mouth. *Ahh. No.* If he yelled mercy, would she release him? He sucked in a fervent breath. He wanted her. More than anything now…to become part of her. He tugged at her hair, gently pulling her away. She shook her head, tasting him, then she nipped him. His body jerked, and he fell back on his elbows. She followed him, tasting him, pleasuring him with her mouth. He shook and his muscles threatened to lock up. *No. No more.*

He opened his mouth…no sound…no words…he had nothing. He tugged at her hair, harder. She released him and flipped the edge of her hair over one shoulder, peering up at him when he rose on his knees.

Neil shook his head and pointed a finger at her. "Don't move," he ordered and kicked off the rest of his clothing. He whipped his shirt over his head and paused.

His gaze dipped, scanned her from her toes to her eyes and grinned. *Those eyes melted him faster than chocolate.* Like freshly baked cookies, he was going to enjoy every little flavor she offered. Crouching at her feet, he lifted her leg and kissed her ankle, then her calf to her knee. Her eyes widened as he placed a quick kiss against her curls, then continued up her belly, to her breasts. He drew a nipple into his mouth, savoring the flavor once more along with the sigh. Neil nipped harder, and Hannah bowed off the bed with a deep moan of satisfaction. He replaced his mouth with his callused hand, pinching the same nipple as he nipped the other, hard, crawling in between her legs, spreading them with the width of his hips.

He lifted his gaze to her eyes. "You sure?"

"Yes, damn it," she hissed.

"Wait. Protection." He leaned over reaching for his wallet.

Hannah's legs tightened. "No, it's good. I'm on birth control, and I had a clean record on my last check-up. You? Please say you're clean too," she begged.

"I'm clean. I always wear protection," he ground out.

"Always?"

"Always."

Neil gazed at her and let the edges of his mouth lift while he plunged into her. Her hips jerked up, and she gasped. He stopped, still deep inside.

"Too much?"

"No. No, so good," she panted through slightly parted lips.

He chuckled, pulled out slightly, and slammed home again and again. Her moans and his grunting fell into the rhythm of their bodies. He kissed her hard as heat ripped at him drawing him tight. She ran her nails down his back, resting one hand on his hips, then pulling him closer, urging him on. Hannah was a wildfire that called to him, and he lifted himself, increasing the pace. Her whimpers fed his own lust, causing it to scale higher and higher and finally, she arched beneath him, gripping Neil while her body milked him in her spasms of release. She was so beautiful, and he let go with the last of her cries, pressing himself deep and roared his own release. His muscles quivered, and he breathed heavily. Finally, he rolled off his delightful and seductive chef, flopped on his back, and pulled Hannah to his side. *Mine.*

****

Morning light filled the room. Hannah shifted and snuggled closer to the warmth of the body next to her. Her muscles ached, and she bit back a grin. Forcing her body not to shake, she continued breathing softly while the scenes of the evening floated in her mind. Neil had handled her in a way that made her feel like she was a petite size four instead of a twelve. Warmth climbed up her neck as she remembered her own demands during their second—or was it third—round of lovemaking?

"I'm awake, and if you keep twitching like that, I'm not going to be nice and let you sleep in."

Neil's deep voice caused a short burst of electricity to vibrate inside Hannah's body. She couldn't stop the giggle bubbling out. When he lunged for her, she scrambled toward the side of the mattress, only to be grabbed and pulled back into the middle, and his body landed on hers. His reaction now pressed against her lower belly. She pursed her lips and squinted at him. "What in Heaven's name do you think you're doing?" She pushed against his chest in a halfhearted way. "I need to shower."

He dropped down to bump his nose against hers. "Want some help?"

She laughed when she rose. "Only if you promise to behave."

Neil rolled onto his back. "Well, then, I guess I'll wait. I won't make promises I can't keep."

Hannah spun away before he could see her frown. *Was what happened between them just sex?* She grabbed her shirt off the floor, wielded it in front of her, and walked into the vanity area. After shutting the door, she dug out a change of clothes, and rushed into the bathroom to turn on the water. Hanging a towel nearby, she got in, then, and only then, did she consider what happened.

She hung her head and wrapped her arms around her waist. It should've been a physical release…a brief escape from all the stress. *Pick up your big girl panties and admit it. It was more than sex for her.* He'd been so gentle. Drat, she was in a pickle now. She heaved a deep sigh and picked up the body wash. Her hand jerked when the shower door slid open, and Neil stepped in behind her. She stiffened.

He took the wash and sponge from her. "Let me do this. I promise I'll behave."

His gentle hands rubbed the sponge along her back. Her muscles relaxed as he lathered her body from behind. She melted against him when he slid his hands across her skin to slowly massage her breasts, then her belly. She allowed the warmth to spread through her.

Although his body responded to her closeness, he continued to wash her gently and methodically. Hannah sighed. When he was finished, Neil dropped the sponge and stepped forward to place them both under the shower spray. His fingers stroked her head while he lifted strands of her hair, rinsing it under the water.

Her heart softened while they stood there allowing the water to pour over them.

"My turn," she whispered.

Chapter Thirteen

Neil opened the passenger door for Hannah while the crisp air bit at his skin. He scanned her face. She ignored him, her back ramrod straight. He jogged around to the driver's door. *She's pissed.* W*hy? What'd he do now? He'd behaved during their shower even when it cost him nearly every ounce of control he owned.* He got in and notched up the heater.

"How's it warm in here already?" she asked.

"I ran out and cranked it on while you were cooking." His chest tightened as her lavender scent surrounded him in the car. He wanted her again.

"Thank you. At the rate you're going, you should have this place all done soon."

He shrugged. "Only the cosmetics. There's a bunch of structural work yet to be done, but it's solid until spring."

Silence.

Neil swallowed past the lump in his throat. "You know it's safe here. I wish you'd consider moving here until the killer is caught."

"I know."

"I could use your input on the kitchen remodeling since you're a chef and all." *Damn it. Lame excuse.*

"I don't have to live here to give you input. Besides, I need my car. I don't think it's wise to move in with you, even for a short time."

Her phone rang. He clamped his lips shut and started driving while she spoke to her caller. It was the shop. Her car would be there a few days. *Okay, that's good.* Whoever followed her wouldn't recognize a rental if she got one.

She hung up and shifted in her seat.

He glanced her way. "You need a rental."

"Yes, and they're coming to pick me up at my place at three."

"Why? I can drive you there."

"Don't you have work today? Or do detectives make their own hours?"

Neil scowled. "It's not like that. I do have work, but I can work in the office or from home, if needed. I think you should reconsider staying with me. No one knows where my house is. It's not far from anything." *Blast it. No begging.* He cleared his throat and shrugged. "It's only a suggestion."

"I appreciate it. I mean it. But I'm not going to run scared every time something like this happens. I am glad you helped me this weekend. But I need to get to my own things. I've got an appointment in two weeks for another roommate. I need to get the place ready."

"Another roommate? What's wrong with the one you have?"

She gazed out the window and said nothing.

"Hannah?"

"What?"

"You have a roommate. Why are you interviewing for another?"

She pointed out the front windshield. "We're here. Please park up close."

He pulled into the farthest parking spot available,

shut off the car, and twisted to face her. He grabbed her hand. "What's going on?"

She frowned out the window and then at his hand. She tugged her arm away, and he released her. "Nothing. I don't have to explain everything to you, you know. Just because we had sex, doesn't mean I have to tell you everything now."

"Just because we... I see." His gut burned. He cranked on the engine, sped toward the front, and slammed on the brakes. "There you go, sweetheart."

Hannah grabbed her things before slamming the door and running up the stairs to her apartment. What on earth was she hiding? He'd practically begged her to stay with him. No other woman had received such an invitation. Hell, he wanted to fix up the kitchen for her.

Damn it. He had to keep her safe. He scanned the parking lot. Hannah's neighbor and his boy stepped out of their place chatting. They didn't seem to notice him. He could be a stalker, and they barely registered his presence. *Hell.* Maybe he could talk them into being more alert. Maybe he could convince the father to check in on Hannah. Maybe he should quit grasping for ideas and man up to do the work himself.

Neil slumped back and growled at his dashboard. *Fine*. He sat up and pulled out his phone. He'd protect her on his own. He glanced at the clock. There was time to get the guys he'd hired started on delivering his apartment items and come back here to wait. He'd done stakeouts before. No big deal. He relocated to the back part of the lot. As long as he could see her door, it'd work. If Hannah didn't spot him.

****

Hannah emptied her dishwasher while last night's

activities played in her mind. Her body tingled, and she shivered. She paused and closed her eyes—recalling the events leading up to those delicious moments. The power outage and the weird moaning had scared the heck out of her. But who wouldn't get frightened experiencing all that within hours of being followed? Likely it was the wind as Neil suggested.

And then this morning, he had to ask about her roommate. How could she explain Rose? How could she explain her panic making her hear moaning in the middle of the night? She couldn't explain. *Not now. Not yet.*

She grabbed a cup of coffee and shuffled toward the living room to drop on the couch. If she hadn't already been tense from the strange car and the frustration at being forced to stay at Neil's house, she might not have overreacted to the odd noises. She stiffened and stood. His house was haunted. That had to be the reason. Did he know?

Hannah laughed. He'd likely dismiss it as his imagination. Mr. Tough Guy probably didn't believe in ghosts. Her phone rang and she answered.

"Hannah?"

"Yes?"

"This is Chef Patterson, I have some bad news," he said.

Hannah's hands tightened on the phone, and she dropped back onto the couch. Her heart pounded. "What is it?"

"Chuck Anderson has passed away. I just got off the phone with his sister, and the doctors confirm it's due to arsenic poisoning. This is gone from allergy issues to something more sinister. I'm telling you this as I know how much the competition means to you.

"Are you saying they're cancelling the competition?"

"No. The competition is still on. However, the school has been temporarily closed pending further investigation. You should expect a call from the police. The administrators are looking at whether to hold the competition at another venue or school…or at all."

"Is there any idea of how long the closure will last?"

"No idea. But I'll still be working there and helping with the investigation. I'll keep you posted, okay?"

Hannah nodded, then cleared her throat. "Okay, thank you, Chef. I appreciate it." As soon as she hung up, her phone rang again. "Hello?"

"Ms. Lincoln?"

"Yes?"

"I'm calling about your car. It's going to take another day for the repairs. The fuel line needed is out of stock here at the local warehouse. I had to order you a replacement."

"I see. Please let me know as soon as it's ready."

"Sure thing… Um…there's something else."

"What is it?"

"Ms. Lincoln, you should know your fuel line showed no signs of deterioration. I looked at it closer, and it's been cut. I'm putting it in a bag for you to pick up when you come get your car or earlier, if you'd like. I think you should know someone wanted your car to die."

"I understand. Thank you." She disconnected and dropped her head in her hands. *Cut. Die.* Everyone else was being poisoned...so why this? Why her? She shuddered, and her chest tightened. She was on the list. Hannah covered her mouth and scanned her apartment. She hadn't checked all the rooms when she arrived home. Granted, she'd only been there an hour or so. What if the person who tried breaking in had come back while she was at Neil's? What if they were in the apartment now? Her lungs clutched the breath she'd inhaled, and her frantic gaze stumbled through her apartment while her heart beat double time. She rubbed her hands on her thighs. *Think.*

She jumped up and ran into the kitchen, grabbed her large butcher knife, and picked her way down the hall toward her bedroom on quivering legs. She should have stayed at Neil's. At least there, she'd have protection. *Should've, would've, could've. Breathe.*

She darted her gaze around as she tiptoed into her bedroom. Nothing looked out of place. Her bathroom door was closed along with Rose's room. *Don't be stupid. At least get someone on the phone, in case. Think.* Hannah dashed back into the kitchen and punched in Neil's phone number. She peered out her front window, and a dark brown van circled her parking lot. She held her breath. Her stomach clenched as if it contained a bag of ice cubes. *Answer the darn phone.* On the third ring, the van circled again, slowing near the bottom of the stairs that led to her apartment. *Oh, heck, no.*

****

Neil pointed to the back room on the bottom floor.

"Buck, that's where I want the boxes stacked. I'll go through them myself and put the stuff where I need it."

"No problem, dude. My cousin Ken just called, and they're five minutes away. He and my brother they'd gonna help me out today. We'll get everything unloaded for you, and you should be set," Buck said, scanning the space. "This place is a lot bigger than your apartment."

"Yeah, I know."

"Ken's got another job tomorrow, but I got my cousin David coming to help me empty your storage unit for you first thing. If you're not here, where you want us to put those things?"

"If there's room, back with the boxes. If not"— Neil studied the main floor—"in here's fine. There's also a third bedroom upstairs that's completely empty. Put the artwork in there."

"Sounds like a plan," he said. "And, hey, I appreciate the job. The extra money's sure to make the old lady happy."

Neil stared at the man. "You still keeping your nose clean? I don't want to see you back on the streets."

"I'm keeping clean and going to my meetings too. I'm not going to let you down."

"Do a good job, and I might be able to find you some more work."

Buck lifted his hands and grinned. "I promise. This will be done like professionals."

"Better be," Neil said and strode toward the kitchen when his phone rang. He pulled it out and recognized Hannah's number. He punched the answer button.

"Hey, honey. I should be there in about an hour to replace the locks," he said with a grin.

"Neil."

Her voice quivered, and his gut clenched. He ran

out of the house. "What's going on? I'm on my way."

"I didn't say—"

"I hear it in your voice, sweetheart. Now, tell me what's wrong," Neil ordered while he jumped in his car and cranked the engine. *Crap*. His shoulders tightened when the line stayed quiet.

She whispered something.

He punched the gas. "Say that again. I didn't catch it."

"I said there's a dark brown van circling my parking lot, and I forgot to check the whole apartment when I arrived. I'm standing in my kitchen with a butcher knife, shaking like a leaf."

"Listen to me, carefully. I want you to go to your neighbor's place. The man and boy I met before...the one you make cookies for. Go and wait there for me. I'll be there in"—he glanced at the dash clock—"twelve minutes. And Hannah?"

"Yes?"

"Leave everything in your apartment, even the knife. Don't hang up. "

"Mr. Turner and his son, Billy's apartment is down the stairs, and last time I looked, the van slowed down near the bottom of the steps."

Damn it to hell.

"Okay, make it obvious you're talking on the phone when you go down. Time it so they're on the other side of the lot before you open your door. Run if you have to. Just get inside your neighbor's apartment. Wait. Are they home?"

"Yes. I talked to them yesterday, and they were chatting about doing a movie marathon today."

"Good. Now, watch and go."

He whipped his car around the next corner and sped up. His hand clenched the steering wheel while Hannah's breathing echoed in his ear. His chest tightened, and he forced air in and out of his lungs.

"You still there, sweetheart? Talk to me."

"The van just passed. Okay, I'm opening the door and running down the stairs."

Neil's heart kicked up a notch while her quick steps echoed in his ears. His hands gripped the wheel tighter as sounds of knocking kicked through the phone.

"I'm at the Turners. Oh, hey there, how are you? Can we talk inside?"

Neil waited while the young boy answered, and the closing of the door echoed across the line. *She's in.* He let out a breath and pulled into the parking lot of Hannah's building ten minutes after she'd disconnected. He drove a loop around the entire building and found no dark brown van. *Crap.*

Chapter Fourteen

Hannah peered through the blinds until Neil's car parked alongside the sidewalk. She nodded at Mr. Turner, who stood watch with her. Neil met her at the bottom of the stairs, and after checking her over, he grabbed her hand, and they bounded up to her apartment, leaving Mr. Turner and his son to scan the lot.

"Pack enough to last you a few weeks. You're staying with me until we get this figured out and no arguing," Neil said.

Like she'd argue now? Bravery had flown out the window when she spotted the dark van skulking the apartment building. Her heart pounded as she nodded and followed Neil. They paused at the front door, and he raised his hand.

"Wait out here while I clear it. If anything happens, run back down to the Turner place."

She wrapped her arms around her middle and scanned behind and around. No movements…no dark van. If Mr. Turner hadn't seen it, she'd have thought she imagined it. Not now, though. It was real. She shivered.

"Clear."

She jumped at Neil's voice, and spun around to rush inside. She grabbed her suitcase and threw in everything she could grab. Lifting her backpack, she checked the contents. Everything there. She glanced around her apartment, looking for anything she might have missed. Nothing. She rushed past Neil standing at her front door and into the kitchen. Pulling out a cooler bag, she stashed items from her fridge and cooking supplies. Comfort items. She returned and faced Neil, who remained by her door watching the apartment property. His back toward her, she took a moment and studied his body. Yep, security and total heat, all in one. She tapped him on the shoulder.

"Ready?" he asked without turning around.

"Yes," she replied and stepped outside.

"Stand beside me and don't move." He locked the door and jiggled the keys. "Let's drop these off with your neighbor."

"Okay," she replied.

He took her hand, and they descended the steps together.

After explaining to Mr. Turner what was going on and promising Billy more cookies, Hannah settled back inside Neil's car. Without a word, he turned the car around and shot out of the lot. She waited for him to say something, anything. As the silence grew, she shrugged and stared out the window.

She frowned. "It's not like I own a gun or anything to protect myself."

Neil scowled at her. "Most who own a gun shouldn't anyway."

"I wouldn't just go out and buy one. I'd learn how to use it first."

"Are you willing to point it at another human being and shoot them? Are you willing to kill?"

"What?" she asked.

"Exactly," he spat out.

Why was he angry at her? It wasn't like she asked for this to happen. Her back straightened, and she twisted in her seat and faced him.

"Listen, if you'd rather I didn't stay with you, I can always go to my parents' house."

"Not happening."

She blew out a breath. "Why not? I'd be safe there."

"Not happening. You're staying with me, and we're not arguing about it," he snapped.

She opened her mouth to *argue* when his phone rang. He answered, and she turned back to stare out the window.

"I did some checking on him, too. He looks good for it. Thanks for the confirmation, Jordan. We'll keep him in our sights," Neil said.

Hannah glanced at him. Who was he talking about? Was this about her? She scanned his face and couldn't tell anything by his stony look.

"What gift?" He shook his head. "No, I don't need that…really."

Gift? She held her breath trying to hear the other part of the conversation.

"Fine. Fine. This weekend? Can't it wait? How about if I just pay—fine."

She let out her breath. She couldn't hear anything on the other end of the phone. She shifted and regarded the view from the window, catching the last few words he spoke.

"The administrator already gave us the green light. We'll run it as soon as the captain clears us."

When he hung up, she asked him, "What was that

about?"

"We're setting up an op to catch the killer."

Hannah leaned forward. "An op? Who do you think it is?"

Neil glanced at her. "Tarnekes."

"Really? Wayne? Are you sure?"

Neil jerked his shoulder. "He's had several run-ins with the police and other things I can't talk about."

"And the administration agreed to this op thing? Will it affect the competition?"

They arrived at Neil's house, and he hit the brakes. "The competition?" He twisted in his seat and grabbed her arm. "That's all you're worried about?"

"No, no." *Drat it.* "I don't want to see anyone else get hurt…or killed. I keep hoping this is all just coincidence."

"Hannah."

Her shoulders slumped. "What I'm saying is that if it isn't a coincidence, they should cancel the competition so no one else gets hurt."

He grabbed her bags and headed inside. She ran after him. Blasted man. She found him placing her bags in the master bedroom next to the bed. The bed. He'd had furniture brought in. *Stop.* She planted her fists on her hips and stationed herself in the doorway to block him. "You seriously don't think I care only about the competition, do you?"

"You're spouting words to that effect," he retorted.

"That's not what I mean. I can survive if the competition is cancelled. I'll handle it somehow. It's not worth people dying for."

"But it's important to you."

"Of course, it is. I've told you why."

Neil sat on the edge of the bed and patted the mattress next to him. She sat close, and he wrapped his arm over her shoulders.

"No, you haven't. Not all of it, so tell me now."

Hannah stared at the floor. How to explain how important this competition was to her so he'd understand? Her body warmed being near him. His scent filled her nose, and her body tingled. How could she explain anything when he affected her like this? She pushed down her body's reaction. She had no choice.

"My parents raised us to be independent. My older brothers raced out on their own and succeeded. Marcus joined the Marines…a fat lot of good that did him." She sighed. "The point is that I want to do this on my own. I want to open my own bakery. Even though my parents have offered to help, I want to show them and myself that I can do this alone."

"Accepting help doesn't mean giving up your independence."

"I know that. I've accepted your help in this protection thing."

"You don't have a choice there, sweetheart."

Hannah jerked then jumped up. "Yes, I do. If I wanted to leave now, I could. I still have that rental car reserved."

Neil rose to stand close. His voice dropped. "I'll handcuff you to the bed if I have to. You're not going anywhere without me until we catch this killer."

She gasped at the idea of being handcuffed and at his mercy. Her lips pursed. "You'd kidnap me to keep me safe?"

His arms whipped around her and jerked her body

against his. He dipped his head, and his mouth claimed hers. Her mind blanked at his assault, and she shivered. She wrapped her arms over his shoulders and kissed him back with every frustrated nerve she had. His lips moved on hers and opened to delve inside. Their tongues danced while his hips rocked against her.

He trailed soft kisses across her cheek to her ear. His voice was gravelly, as he whispered, "I'll do anything to keep you safe, love."

"Neil." Hannah pressed against him. "If I'm going to stay here, I need to cancel the rental."

Neil twisted and tugged her over him as he dropped on the bed. "Later," he whispered, and ran his tongue across her collar bone.

She wiggled. Her body aching for his. "It'll only take a minute."

"Woman." He flipped over and trapped her between his hard body and the mattress. Her mind blanked.

****

The next morning, Neil rolled over when a soft laugh woke him. He sucked in a breath, watching Hannah breathe steady and slow. Good, the ghost hadn't awakened her. He touched her bare shoulder and caressed her exposed skin, leaning close to inhale her scent. Scenes of their recent lovemaking trickled in his mind, and his body hardened. He wanted her again. She had a hold on him he couldn't shake. Her warmth called to him, but he leaned away from her. After the excitement of yesterday and last night's activities, she needed rest. He rubbed his hand over his face and blew out a breath.

Quietly, he slid off the bed and tossed on a pair of

sweats. He slipped the door closed and headed down the stairs. In the kitchen, a hazy image of Muriel solidified. She pursed her lips and shook her finger at him.

"You had best make an honest woman of that girl. She's too special to treat badly. My dear husband would never have expected relations before the wedding." She giggled and floated near the stove. "Mind you, he had hands that—"

"No, no. Don't tell me," Neil ordered. *Blast it.* That's all he needed to hear. He peered above the cabinets, but nothing was there. He'd already checked and cleared the place. There had to be something to explain the woman. Hallucinations, maybe? *Damn it.* He'd inspected inside yesterday and confirmed no hidden cameras or microphones.

"You're going to have to accept it. I'm never leaving."

"Why not? The house is in good hands, and that should be enough. If you really are what you say you are."

"And leave you to your own devices with that lovely girl? I think not." She shimmered and solidified closer to him. "I mentored the Young Ladies Magnolia Club in my day. There are always ways to help a woman acclimate to married life."

"Married life?" Neil cringed. The room started to spin, and he dropped onto the nearest stool. *Married?*

"Who are you talking to?" Hannah asked.

Neil jumped up and spun around. "What?"

Hannah squinted at him and scanned the kitchen. The corners of her lips lifted, and her eyebrows rose.

"I asked who you were speaking to."

He shifted his gaze away from her alluring body hugged snugly by his T-shirt. "Umm…myself."

"Really?" She strode around him and ran her hands along the countertop. "I love this kitchen and the granite. Did I tell you that already?"

He studied her and then bit his lip when Muriel appeared behind Hannah. He tipped his head to the side and frowned.

"You don't like it?" Hannah asked.

Pay attention, man. "Yes, I like it now that I've got the granite and cabinet doors installed. I have the small appliances being shipped in a few days.

Hannah nodded. "It's very roomy." She shifted and opened the fridge. "Wow, fairly sparse in here."

"I haven't gone to the grocery store yet."

She pulled out eggs and deli ham. "If you have some spices, I can whip us up an omelet."

He pointed to the thin cabinet next to the stove. "In there is what I have."

While Hannah cooked, he set out plates and silverware. She'd overheard him talking to Muriel and didn't go running. Did she think he'd lost it?

"If I'm going to be staying here," she said over her shoulder, as she slipped the omelets onto the plates, "we're going to have to do a store run. What I've brought isn't going to be enough, even combined with your meager stash."

"Sure, no problem," he agreed.

After they ate and cleared the plates, Hannah touched his arm and waved at the furniture stacked in the living room. "Where did all this come from? I know it wasn't at your apartment."

"I've had it in storage."

"You've collected furniture?"

"No, they're gifts from my mother."

"Your mother sends you furniture?"

"They're antiques. She's a dealer." He frowned.

"I'm assuming all the artwork I spotted in the guest room is also from her?"

He nodded, and his stomach burned. "She thinks to buy me with it, and I've stuck it in storage this whole time."

"I see."

"Do you?"

"Yes, why not? I'm assuming your relationship with her isn't the best, and this is her way of trying to extend an apology of sorts?"

"Maybe. Who knows with her."

Hannah tilted her head. "You don't want to make things right with her? She's your mother."

"So, why does Rose call every night? She doesn't have anyone else?"

Hannah pursed her lips, sat, and clasped her hands together. "I'll tell you about Rose, if you'll promise to keep an open mind."

"Why do you think I won't?"

She grinned. "You really want to know?"

Neil scowled. "Tell me about her."

She leaned forward onto the island and stared out the window. "Last summer, I decided to get a roommate. I had received a call from Rose and we met. We hit it off immediately. Her major was Criminal Law." Her voice trembled when she spoke.

"Was?" Neil asked.

"Yes."

"She dropped out?"

"No. Not exactly."

There's something she's not saying. He inhaled slowly and waited.

"Rose decided to park in the west lot one night. It's not lit very well, and it's a longer path to and from class. But the east lot had been full, and she didn't want to miss class. Plus, she hadn't received her parking tags, yet." Hannah glanced at him.

"Go on," he encouraged.

"Well, that night, she called to talk to me while walking to her car, and I missed her call." Hannah's eyes filled with tears.

Oh no. Tears. No tears. He leaned over and hugged her to him.

She sniffed and spoke in a ragged whisper, "That night, Rose was attacked and killed near her car."

Neil stilled. *Killed. Wait…last summer?* "Hannah, what are you trying to say?"

She pulled out of his arms and stood. "I'm saying I get a call from Rose every night since the night after she died, and I talk to her until she gets in her car."

She's serious. His stomach clenched. "How can you talk to her if she's dead?"

"Well, that's the thing. It's her ghost and she knows it, but we can't figure out how to get her to move on…or do whatever it is that ghosts do to leave here. At least, we couldn't figure it out until I spoke with Victoria."

"Marcus's lady? The ghost hunter?"

"Spirit seeker, yes. So how did you know about her? I contacted her last week, and she explained that I need to go out to the lot and try to see if I can help Rose get past the trauma of her death."

"Marcus mentioned her to me. How the hell are you supposed to help Rose do that?"

"Well, see, Rose can't remember anything until the time she calls and then hangs up. So, if I'm there in person, maybe we can get her to see what happened...or remember what truly happened, and it might help her."

"You're serious."

"Of course, I am. I'm telling you because I want to go out there. But I don't want to go alone. Not now, with everything that's happened."

"That's smart...the not going out alone part."

"You don't believe me," she said, her hands clenching.

"I believe that you believe." *Would that work? What a damn mess.*

"Forget it. Forget I said anything."

"No, I won't. Listen, I've been with you when your phone rings, so I know someone is calling you. I'm not sure if I can wrap my head around it being a ghost."

"And, dear boy, why not?" Muriel asked.

Neil stiffened. *Nope. Not going there.*

"You hear me quite well, and yet...you doubt this one who holds your heart?"

"I'll go with you. I'm not sure how it'll help, but if you feel this strongly about it, then I'll go and protect you."

"Even if you don't believe me?"

"It's not a matter of believing what you're saying. I said I'll come with you, and I will. Just don't ask for me to believe in woo-woo stuff, okay?"

"Woo-woo stuff?"

"You know what I mean."

"I'm wondering if I do." Hannah got up and walked away.

"Where are you going now?" Neil asked and rushed after her.

"I'm taking a shower and packing. Since I cancelled the rental yesterday, I'll need a ride. I'm going to my parents' house to think about all this," she said over her shoulder.

Crap.

****

An hour later, Hannah and Neil got on the road north. When they arrived at her parents' house, she discovered her brother Marcus had invited Victoria. She'd caught the looks they shared. There was more going on between them than they let on. *Good.* She had to stop worrying about him and focus on her own problems.

She leaned in to speak softly to her brother. "Your month is up."

Marcus's eyes widened. "Hannah—"

"But you are doing so much better now. I can tell," she interrupted then continued, "So no pressure here, brother. She's healing you, and because I love you, I don't care that it's her and not us." She narrowed her eyes. "Do you understand what I'm saying?"

He nodded, then slid his glance toward Neil and back to Hannah. "Where's that going?"

Hannah shifted and studied Neil. They stared at each other for a few moments before she turned back to Marcus.

"I'm not exactly sure." She continued in a low voice, "No, that's a lie. It'll likely end where I think it will. It's sure to be a complicated path, though."

"Be careful. He rubs me the wrong way, and I can't read him," her brother warned.

"That, brother mine, is the crux of our problems," she said. Neil was a hard man to understand.

Marcus laid his hand over hers on the table. "I'm here. Even messed up, you're not alone."

Hannah grinned. "I know. Thanks, but I'll figure it out."

He nodded and turned to Victoria.

"That's so fascinating, Victoria," Hannah's mom crowed. "I'm so sorry to hear about the fire. But from what you've told me, I think you'll be extremely successful once you do open your business. Most people are afraid more than anything. Knowledge can help ease their insecurities. I'm a staunch believer that education erases a lot of our fears. You have such a smart point of view."

"In fact, Mrs. Lincoln—" Victoria glanced at Marcus. He gave her a nod, and she continued. "I was out in your garden earlier today and noticed a presence."

Hannah sat forward. This was interesting.

"Really?" Mom glanced between Marcus and Victoria. "Do you know who it is?"

"Not yet. Marcus will be going out there with me later to introduce ourselves. But before we do, I thought I'd ask you if you had any idea who it might be?" Victoria asked.

Mom shook her head.

Victoria was talking about ghosts. Who would be out in the garden? Hannah bit her lip to keep from interrupting and asking again about Rose immediately.

"Well, then. We'll have to see who it is," Victoria

announced.

"Can we come, too, or will too many people be an issue?" Hannah's father asked.

Yes, good idea. Hannah crossed her fingers under the table.

Victoria grinned. "It seemed like the spirit is a cautious one. It might not manifest with a large audience. Since she didn't mind Marcus's presence the first time, I believe there won't be a problem with him there again as well."

"Makes sense," Mom responded. "Besides, you'll be doing this later tonight, won't you?"

"Yes, much later. I usually find the best time to do these things near a large group is when everyone has already settled in for the night," Victoria explained.

"Well, that settles that. We'll be in bed asleep. But first thing in the morning, you'll give us a report, yes?" Mom requested.

"Of course."

The conversation around the table switched to the events surrounding Hannah's externship with her school and the latest update on the competition. She bit her lip to keep from frowning directly at Neil. If he hadn't got involved, the competition wouldn't be in jeopardy. To be fair, if he hadn't got involved, she might have become a victim. His presence had to be the reason she wasn't hurt. Yet.

Neil sat still, speaking rarely. Hannah caught him staring at her throughout the conversation when he wasn't focused on Victoria. What did he want? Later. She'd figure it out later. At this moment, Victoria had her attention as well.

She'd be a great resource in getting more details on

what to do for Rose. She'd have to catch her at a free moment. If her brother would stop stalking the girl, she'd have that moment. Maybe tomorrow she'd catch her for a few minutes. With that idea, Hannah got to her feet.

"Since I can't join the fun in the garden, I'm headed to bed. It's been a long week."

Neil got up as well. "I've got a couple calls to make before hitting the sack. Is the couch available?"

Hannah slid a glance underneath her lashes. *Good boy.*

"Of course it is. But since the other kids aren't here, why don't you take Conner's room?"

"Conner?" Neil asked.

"My eldest son. Follow me and you can get settled in," Mom advised before heading down the hall.

Neil shot a quick frown at Hannah before turning to follow the older woman.

Hannah shrugged, then her phone rang. *Rose.*

Chapter Fifteen

Hannah flipped over for the fourth time since the sunlight filtered through the curtains announcing the beginning of the day. She blew out a breath and swung her legs over the side of the bed and stood. Aromas of fresh bacon and pancakes hit her, and her stomach grumbled its need. She aimed for the shower. As the water sprayed over her face, the dreams of last night flashed in her mind. Her body ached while the memories of her fantasy floated in and out of her head. She shivered. *Neil.*

She stepped out and dried off, taking a deep breath. Breakfast called her. Was Victoria an early riser? Rushing to finish dressing, Hannah skipped downstairs and paused at the kitchen entrance. Victoria sat at the island drinking coffee and chatted with Hannah's mom. Grabbing a cup of coffee, she joined them.

"Good morning," Victoria greeted her.

"Good morning," she said. "If you have a few minutes, I'd like to talk to you a little more about Rose?"

"Of course."

"You two go out on the back porch and chat. The men will be here shortly, and you don't want to be interrupted," Hannah's mom warned.

They headed out and after settling down, Hannah leaned forward. "I've been thinking about your advice regarding Rose since our phone conversation. I have a few more questions," she said setting her cup on the table.

"Go ahead," Victoria responded before taking a sip of coffee.

"If I understood you correctly, I need to help Rose move on. I get it. My concern is once we're in the parking lot and I'm waiting for her to call. How do I see her? Or, am I going to see her? If I do, how do I help her get past the attack?"

Victoria smiled, set her cup down, and patted Hannah's arm. "Let me start by explaining everyone has guides, for lack of a better word. You know when you're walking down the street and for some odd reason a thought pops in your head to go left instead of right?"

Hannah nodded, ignoring the tingle down her back. She picked up her cup again, wrapping her fingers around it for warmth.

"That is your guide telling you which way to go. Your friend, Neil, calls his guide his gut or instinct. It's safer for non-believers to think of it that way, rather than admit they have a spiritual guide helping them."

"I see," Hannah said. *Makes sense.*

"Okay, now, when you go to the parking lot to help Rose, I suggest you clear your mind and follow your guide. The best way to do it, is to listen to whatever message pops in your head. For example, if you're standing there and for one reason or other, the idea of walking to your left comes to mind. Walk left." Victoria paused a moment, then continued. "If you keep your mind clear and accept what messages are coming to you, then you are more likely to see something. If you see anything, a shadow, a mist…anything which seems *off*, don't dismiss it. It could be Rose trying to reach out."

"Okay, but if I don't see her? How do I know what to do?"

"She'll still call, yes?"

"Yes," Hannah assured Victoria. Rose always called.

"Then while she's on the phone, let her know you're with her. Not all spirits are aware they need to manifest for the living to see them. Ask her to try to let you see her. If it doesn't work, it's okay. But, tell her she must stay on the phone the entire time. You know how things occurred that night?"

"Yes, I had a friend read the police report. It looks like she was attacked after class in the parking lot the moment she reached her car."

"Then you need to have her give you details of her car, her walking to her car, and opening the door. Tell her to describe everything she's seeing and doing. Don't let her go through her routine of talking to you as you've done in the past. This needs to be different. For her to remember and break the cycle, she needs to get past the point of simply opening her doors. In her phone calls, you said she ends the call once she's in the car, correct?"

"Yes. But, according to the police, she never got in the car."

"Exactly. Think about that for a minute," Victoria suggested.

Shoot. How could she have missed that? Hannah's eyes widened. "It's not a replay of that last night."

"No, it is," she said and leaned back before

continuing, "She's altered her memory and kept it going like a rerun of a movie. It needs to play out exactly how things happened for her to realize the alternate memory is incorrect."

"Why would she create an alternate memory?" Hannah asked.

"The same reason we, the living, do." Victoria spread her hands. "To hide from reality."

Hannah dipped her chin. "That's so sad."

"What happened to her is sad."

"True. I understand. I really appreciate you explaining this to me. Will we see the attack?" Hannah shuddered.

Victoria leaned forward, grinning. "You said 'we.' Does that mean Neil will be joining you?"

"He's decided the best way of being my body guard, is if he's with me as often as possible. I guess it means he'll be there too, since I doubt he'd let me go out to a darkened parking lot, at night, alone."

"Good. Now, I can't promise you won't see the attacker or the attack. Be prepared in case it happens, though. The best thing to remember is, this is more like a movie and you're hitting a pause button. You may see the attack, but you won't be attacked. You'll be safe. Neil comes across as someone who doesn't believe in the paranormal. But, I think deep down, he's not a complete non-believer."

"Why do you say that?"

"Ladies, breakfast is ready," Neil spoke from the doorway.

Hannah gasped. How long had he been standing there? Did he hear everything?

"Thank you, Neil," Victoria said while she rose.

She shifted and whispered to Hannah, "He didn't hear anything."

She shot Victoria a glance. Good. But, how did she know? Maybe it wasn't better not to ask. During breakfast, Hannah studied Neil as they ate and talked about their plans for the weekend.

"I'm staying through Monday," Hannah responded when her father asked.

Neil glanced at her and then back to the group. "I have to leave. I've got work to do."

Hannah frowned at him. The op, he said they were planning. Great, killer on the loose and the competition likely to be cancelled and there wasn't a thing she could do.

"When is this thing going to happen?"

Neil frowned at her.

"What thing?" Hannah's father asked.

Hannah scowled at Neil before speaking to her father. "An op, apparently," she said, waving a hand. "The police are going to see if they can catch the killer in the act, so to speak."

"They're having another practice session a week from Monday, and since the attacks have occurred during these sessions, we're hoping to catch whoever is doing this," Neil supplied.

"Anyone in particular?" Hannah's father asked.

"Yes, sir. However, I can't talk about it. I hope you understand."

"Of course, if Hannah is safe, I understand."

"Dad," Hannah interrupted. "Neil will be there along with however many other cops. I'm sure I'll be fine. Once they catch whoever it is, then the competition can go on."

"No competition is worth your life, dear," her mother said.

Neil stood. "I agree. I need to head out now."

Hannah nodded and rose, following him to the front door. He swung around, grabbed her, and pulled her close. His mouth swooped down on hers, and heat rushed through her. He backed away and grinned.

"I'll see you soon, honey. Call me when you head out of here," Neil whispered before he pivoted and strode to his car.

She waited for him to drive away before heading back inside. Avoiding the dining room, she rushed upstairs to her room and dropped on the bed, sighing. Hannah stared at the ceiling as her fingertips brushed her lips. The man could sure kiss. Even when he infuriated her, she wanted him. Her heart tripped as images of their time together flashed in her mind. Drat, she'd fallen hard for Neil. Now what?

Chapter Sixteen

Sunday morning Hannah strode into the kitchen as the sun rose, shooting streams of light across her mother's counter. She checked the time. Everyone should be about to rise. She pulled fruit out of the fridge and began cutting it up. Her mother joined her after a few minutes, and started mixing eggs, milk, and cinnamon for dipping.

"French toast and fruit?" her mother asked.

"Sounds perfect," Hannah responded.

"So, tell me about your classes. Not this morbid ordeal on the competition. I'd rather not think about that this morning."

Hannah added the watermelon pieces to the plate and began slicing strawberries. "Well, Chef Patterson is not happy. If this case isn't wrapped up soon, it could affect the school."

"Hannah, classes."

"Sorry, Mom," Hannah said and continued, "Chef Patterson is pushing the sustainability portion of the classwork. He's determined to increase awareness of it in the school, and the local economy is sure to benefit."

"Is he a good instructor?"

"He's one of the best. There's several who are certified with so many letters I dream to achieve at some point in my life," Hannah paused and chuckled. "Oh, then there's Chef Caulder. Poor man can hardly remember anyone's name, yet he can recall every ingredient to every recipe he teaches. It's amazing and odd."

"Chef Caulder? That's not a popular last name." Her mother paused and dipped several pieces of bread in the egg mixture before setting them on the cooktop. She wiped her hands and turned. "Do you happen to know where he's from?"

Hannah placed the strawberries on the plate and grabbed a ripe honeydew melon. "I'm not sure. I know he's lived in Georgia all his life, but not sure exactly where. Why?"

"Is his first name John?"

"Yes," Hannah said and stopped cutting to face her mom. "You know him?"

"Describe him to me first," she said and flipped the bread over to brown the other sides of the pieces. The aroma of French toast and fresh fruit filled the kitchen.

"Well, I can't tell his age exactly because he's usually unkempt. Clean, but wrinkled clothes and stooped over. He's close to your age, but his behavior makes him seem older. I think it's because his hair isn't combed often. He has a large nose. I might have a photo of him on my phone, hold on." Hannah stepped to the sink, washing and drying her hands. She ran upstairs and grabbed her phone.

When she returned, her mother had added another batch of toast on the stove and studied the photo Hannah found. Her mother frowned.

"Do you know him?"

Her mother nodded. "Hannah, has he mentioned anything about knowing me?"

"No. I'm surprised…no wait," Hannah paused and

sat on the bar stool. "Mom, he never remembers anyone's name. But, he's called me 'Hilly' since the first day we met."

"Oh dear," her Mom returned and joined Hannah at the counter.

Hannah's father walked in and after glancing at them both, asked "What's wrong?"

She tipped her phone to show him the photo. He frowned and after glancing at her mother sat beside her. "He's one of your instructors?"

"Yes." Her shoulders tensed. "Why? Who is he? How do you know him?"

"He hasn't said anything to her, honey," Hannah's mother offered.

"Who is he?" Hannah asked again.

Her father cleared his throat, patted her shoulder, and nodded to her mother. "You better explain."

"I dated him years ago. Before I met your father. It was quite serious for almost a year. However, your father came along, and I knew I had to break things off with John. He didn't take it well."

Her father scoffed then interjected, "We had to get a restraining order. After that, he disappeared, and we haven't seen him since. Well, not until now."

The hairs on Hannah's neck itched. "He calls me 'Hilly', dad. Mom's name is Hillary. I think he thinks I'm mom."

"He can't believe that. Not at his age. Besides, he married two years after your mother and I did."

"He did?" her mother asked.

"Yes, I kept tabs on him for a bit," her father said.

"Dad?" Hannah asked. "Why?"

"Just to be sure he'd moved on. When I discovered

180

he'd married, I let it go."

"I should probably tell Neil. If he finds out we know this and didn't tell him, he'll be truly ticked off," Hannah stated.

"I agree," her father said. "However, I don't believe it's of any consequence. If he's focused on teaching and he believes you to be your mother, then you've nothing to worry about."

"Why not?"

"Because he loved your mother very much. He'd never hurt her, so it makes sense he wouldn't hurt you."

"True," Hannah replied.

The odor of burning bread filled the kitchen, and her mother jumped up to remove the burning breakfast.

"I'll call Neil and let him know," Hannah said. "Let's not worry about it."

Hannah punched in Neil's number and walked out to the porch when Victoria arrived in the kitchen.

****

Monday morning, Neil finished writing up his report for the captain. The swat team had been assigned, and the school administration was already on board. Security had been updated, and the plan was set.

"I'm telling you Cast, both guys are on the top of my list," Neil said before shifting in his chair and hitting the enter button on his computer.

Cast stood and walked over to Neil's desk to perch on the corner.

"So, we've got two possible suspects here."

"Yeah. You get any more information on that kid?"

His partner shook his head. "Nothing more than we haven't already gathered. Per the research, I did, Chef Caulder has been seeing a counselor ever since his wife died last year. Grief therapy, and he's never missed a support group meeting. I'm leaning more toward the Tarnekes kid. He's got financial troubles, and his parents have been out of the picture since he graduated high school. He's on his own, racking up loans for this school. He's at every session of the competition trials. He'd make a major haul winning."

"Do we know how his skill level is? Does he have a chance to win?"

Cast blew out a breath before answering, "I think they all do to even qualify for the competition." He chuckled. "Who knew cooks could be so competitive?"

"You obviously don't watch some of the cooking channels. It's cut throat out there, from what I've seen."

"You watch the cooking channels?" Cast teased.

Neil scowled. "Yeah, I do. I'm renovating my permanent home. I want a good kitchen and some of those shows give me ideas on how to make use of the space."

"You planning to learn to cook too? Last I heard, you keep to a grill."

"I have cooked a meal once or twice."

"No shit? You got an apron too?"

"Watch it," Neil warned.

"Admit it, you're setting up your kitchen for that woman of yours."

Neil rose and leaned over—his nose now inches from Cast's. "Lancaster, I'm warning you."

Cast barked a laugh which echoed in their office. "Uh huh," he said, and scooted on the other side of the desk. "Deny it all you want, I can see it in your eyes. You're burned from her kind of fire, and it's not going away." He turned and strode out of the office, dodging the wadded paper Neil threw his way and called over his shoulder, "I've got Carrie set up to act as cameraman. I'm going to hit her up for a microphone, and we're making up some press creds."

The door slammed shut, and Neil stared out the back window of his office. Everything had been prepared. He sighed, waiting sucked. He grunted and glanced at the clock. Better that, then Hannah in danger.

Neil grabbed his phone and punched in the little chef's number.

"Hello?"

"How's it going?" The wind picked up outside tearing the final die-hard fall leaves from the oak tree across the street. They danced along the road and disappeared under cars parked in the lot.

"I'm fine. I decided I'm going to stay here until next Monday. I should be safe."

"True. Doubt anyone would drive that far up north to get you. But I should talk to your dad about security, just in case."

"No. Remember, I'm a grown up. I've already talked to him. Neither he nor mom plan on going anywhere, so they'll be here all day. Besides, mom and I have a plum puree to work on. And before you say anything, dad's giving me a ride back home, so I can pick up my car early Monday morning."

"Plum puree? For what?" He frowned and returned to his desk. How'd she know what he was going to ask?

"My recipe for the competition. Do you really want to know the details?"

"No, not really." He grabbed a pen and started doodling.

Silence.

"Can I call you tonight?" And tomorrow tonight and every night until I can see you? Neil glanced at his drawing. Hearts? What the heck? Neil tossed the pen and leaned his head back, closing his eyes.

"Sure." A voice called her name in the background. "I gotta go. I'll talk to you later, okay?"

"You bet." He hung up and stared at the ceiling. At least the woman agreed to stay at her parents until the day of the op. A whole week before he'd see her again. But there was always late-night talks. He grinned and his chest expanded, filling him with warmth. Pictures of Hannah flickered inside his head, and he clenched his jaw. Fire…heat. Yep, she'd gotten him bad. His pulse picked up as his imagination kicked into overtime. Hannah in his kitchen cooking breakfast…cooking dinner…his heart tripped. Hannah cooking oatmeal and cranberry cookies. His cookies. His woman.

Chapter Seventeen

Monday morning, Hannah stood lock-kneed with her back pressed against the wall in the small alcove while her stomach burned. She pressed her hand against her belly and swallowed several times battling the bile clawing for release. She listened to the voices from around the corner and closed her eyes tight. It'd been a week since she saw Neil last at her parents' house. Memories of their nightly calls faded when sounds of policemen reached her.

"Tac team one is standing by out back. Exit doors are covered," the man said as he neared her.

Don't turn the corner. Please.

"Yes, sir, returning now," he said, and his voice lowered when he walked back to the others. He merely glanced at her when he turned, dismissing Hannah.

Inhale. Exhale. She peeked around the corner. Cast held a microphone interviewing one of her competitors. Neil had introduced them earlier. Someone had to have coached him since he asked all the correct questions in his guise of being a reporter. She stared at Neil standing with his long legs spread and hands in pockets like he had no cares. Just a visitor…a boyfriend there to watch his girlfriend practice. They truly expected her to enter that classroom and pretend she wouldn't be standing in the presence of a murderer? She cast a glance in the wide observation windows. Wayne Tarnekes chatted with Chef Caulder. As usual, the older man's head hung down refusing to make eye contact with Wayne.

Hannah shuddered. An actress she never claimed to be, yet, the time had arrived. Straightening her shoulders, she marched around the corner and down the hall toward Neil. He swung around when she approached and grinned at her. How could he be so relaxed? He took her hand before leaning down to kiss her on the cheek.

He whispered in her ear, "Focus on your cooking and leave the rest to me. Nothing is going to happen to you."

She nodded stiffly and moved to enter the room. The noise level increased with excited whispers, and the sounds of pots and pans being set up.

"Once again, you all have two hours to practice your cooking and plating for the competition," Chef Patterson announced. "Ignore the reporters and concentrate. There's a lot riding on this, and you don't want to waste this opportunity you've been given."

A bell rang, and Hannah rushed over to the staple shelving and began gathering her ingredients. She studied the others as she moved from shelf to shelf. *Come on, focus.* Who could focus at a time like this? She took a deep breath, and after setting her ingredients down at her section, moved to the fridge to gather her cold items. When she returned to her station, she jerked. Wayne was assigned to the place across from her. She scanned his ingredients. Nothing in front of him could be considered poisonous, even in large doses. Her breath whooshed out. It wasn't him. Good.

She lifted her chin and rubbed her arms. Only two hours to cook and plate. The competition was too important. *Get it together girl.* Blinking, she pulled her bowls together along with her scale and cups and began measuring ingredients. The room faded into the background while she focused on mixing and cutting. Several pots had already covered the stove when she placed hers on the front burner. Competitors jostled for position to stir or taste their concoctions. Her own wine reduction simmered.

"I'm mixing several fruits. If all you're doing is a reduction, would you mind shifting your pot to the back burner, so I can stand and add to mine?" Carol asked in a low voice.

Hannah nodded and moved her pot. After checking the heat, she moved away to work on the pastry dough. She'd rolled the dough on her counter and prepared to cut slices when the doors flew open. She jerked her head up and everyone started moving.

"Don't move!" Neil's voice shouted.

"Everyone out," Cast followed with a command also. "You by the stove, turn everything off and leave."

Bodies pushed and shoved while some of the women gasped, and Carol's voice pierced through the confusion.

"Don't hurt him," she cried.

Hannah twisted and pushed against the bodies pressing against her to leave the room. She rose on her tip toes and scanned over the heads of the bodies shoving at her. Uniformed policeman with arms spread guided the crowd toward the door. Chef Caulder was pressed up against the far wall with Neil clamping handcuffs on him. *No.* She shoved against the bodies, squeezing between them when she came face to face with a policeman. He shook his head.

"Turn around, miss. You need to leave now," he ordered.

"I'm with Neil…err, Detective Garrett."

"Sorry, ma'am. No one stays. You need to turn around and get out, now," he said, grabbing her arm to keep her from moving past him.

Hannah jerked her arm loose and scowled at him before spinning around and following the crowd. Within minutes, everyone except Neil, Cast, and four officers, were stationed in the hallway staring through the window. Chef Caulder cowed from Neil's handling. The speakers which could be used when new students took a tour had been shut off, so no one could hear what was being said.

The older man pulled and pushed attempting to get away from Neil when Cast stepped in front of him and leaned in close to Chef's face. Whatever he said, Chef stopped moving and stared at him. His glanced shifted, and then he looked straight at Hannah.

****

Hannah shoved through the bodies pressing up against the glass. They wouldn't be taking the chef out the door among the competitors. She ran to the faculty side entrance and tugged on the handle. Locked. Wait. She'd helped Chef Caulder set up the ingredients earlier. She padded her pockets searching for the access key he'd forgotten to take back. She let out a breath when she pulled it from her pocket and swiped it through the magnetic reader. The click echoed loudly in her ears. Grabbing the handle, she whipped open the door and ran down the hallway which led her to the back door of the classroom. She skidded to a stop when the door opened and Cast escorted Chef Caulder through and around the next corner that would lead to the side exit of the building.

They had to have a car parked there. She rushed forth and both Cast, and the chef stopped and turned.

"Wait, please," she pleaded.

Cast scowled at her and raised his hand indicating for her to stop. "Don't come near him. Go back to the others," he ordered.

"Hilly!" Chef Caulder sung out with a large grin on his face. "I knew you'd come back to me. See?" He frowned and shook his head, "But, I'm not done yet." He spat in Cast's face. "You fool! I haven't finished yet. Let me go this instant," he demanded.

"Not yet. We have to ask you a few questions, remember?" Cast said with a flat voice.

"Oh yes, I remember," Chef agreed, and they both turned and left.

Hannah's jaw dropped. He's not done yet? Hilly? He's confused. She jumped when her arm was squeezed and jerked around to face Neil.

His gaze darkened when his sharp voice spat out, "What the hell are you doing here?"

She pulled her arm away. "You're hurting me."

Neil didn't release his grip. She placed a hand on his chest when he shifted and leaned down to stare at her. "You need to leave now. I don't have time for this."

"You don't have time?" She pushed against his chest with no success. He was like a statue made of stone and didn't budge. "Neil, listen to me."

"No, you listen to me. This is a crime scene, and you have no business talking to the suspect. For crying out loud, woman. He just tried to kill you."

"How?" Hannah couldn't stop the question from spilling from her lips.

"How? Who cares about how. He did and that's all there is to it. I'm in charge here, and I should get everything wrapped up. Nothing is going to keep him from going to prison for the rest of his life."

"Neil, wait. He's—"

"Not now, Hannah. This isn't the time or the place," he said, before shifting his glance behind her.

She twisted her head, and a uniformed officer rushed their way.

"I'm sorry, sir. I don't know how she got back here."

"Get her out of here now, Parker." Neil ordered.

"Neil," Hannah pleaded, "Please."

"Ma'am." The officer grabbed her arm and tugged her with him. "This way please."

Hannah tugged her arm away and rushed back to Neil. He clamped a hand on each of her shoulders and spoke to the officer running up behind her, "If she resists, arrest her."

Her mouth dropped open. Neil pivoted and stomped back into the class room. The officer pulled out his handcuffs, and she lifted her brows.

"Seriously?"

"Seriously," the officer responded.

She shook her head and raised her hands in surrender.

"I'm leaving," she said and stomped away. What the heck? Neil wanted to have her arrested when she simply wanted to talk to him? Why wouldn't he listen to her? It was obvious Chef Caulder was unbalanced, even to her.

She shoved open the exit door and continued marching past the crowd out to her car. Once inside, she hit the steering wheel with her fists. Dang it all.

Chapter Eighteen

Several hours later, Hannah stomped into Neil's office and pointed her finger at Cast. "Out," she demanded. Cast glanced at Neil, and at Neil's nod, he grabbed his coat and left, closing the door behind him.

"What on earth do you think you're doing? The competition has been cancelled because of you and this fiasco," the words shot out faster than a semi-automatic.

Neil lifted his shoulder in a half shrug. "I have to go where the information takes me, and this is where it went. I don't think attempted murder can be called a fiasco, honey."

Hannah knocked his name plate onto the floor when she slapped her hands on the top of his desk and leaned forward. "Just like the information took you to believe Tony was a cold-blooded killer?" She laughed bitterly then straightened. "Forgive me if I don't completely trust your ability to do your job. I asked for your help and this is what I get? You've ruined my chances of winning this contest and arrested a man who has no idea of what he's doing."

Neil flattened his lips as he shot up from his chair. His stomach burned, and a band tightened around his chest. "I am a good detective. Tony isn't some innocent kid. He's a felon, dammit."

"Of theft, not murder. There's a huge difference, detective."

"You asked for my help," he countered.

"Yes, but not to get the competition cancelled or hurt an old man," she said, her chest rising and falling rapidly with her anger. "This was my last chance at getting the money to start my business, and you've blown it for me. That on top of what you've done to poor Chef Caulder."

Neil scowled and pointed a finger at her. "That's all this is about isn't it? Money." He waved his arm. "Not the old man or why he did what he did. You only want to prove to your parents you're all grown up and independent. Give it up. You're like every spoiled princess. Get the money from your parents and stop pretending you're something you're not."

Hannah's shoulders jerked, and she took a step back. "That's what you think this is about?" She shook her head. "After all this time, you don't know me or anything about what I want in life. I should have known better."

Her eyes filled with water, and Neil cringed. No tears. Can't...do...tears. He stepped around his desk moving toward her. She backed away.

"No. Don't touch me. Don't console me. I don't want your help anymore. I don't want you around anymore," she said, before whipping around and grabbing the office door. "In fact, I don't want to ever see you again. This last month has been a mistake." She wrenched open the door and paused before leaving, "Stay out of my life."

Neil flinched when the door slammed shut. *What in blazes just happened?* He moved to sit back down and grabbed the case file. Flipping it open, he began reviewing his notes, the investigation reports and then clapped it shut again. What if he was wrong, and Hannah was right? What if he missed something? What if he just quit doing his job? *Hell no.* He didn't need her doubting his ability as a detective. He was a good cop, period. She wasn't getting away with this. He jumped up and ran after her.

His hand slipped between the elevator doors before they could close. He entered and Hannah stood there alone. He waited until the doors shut, then grabbed her shoulders.

"Listen to me. I know how to do my job. The problem here is you want to go around wearing your little rose colored glasses and seeing just puppies and rainbows. You refuse to see what's right in front of you. There was a murderer at your school. You were the next victim. Hell, you're were the next victim if, for no other reason, that you trust too easily! You refuse to see the bad in people. The old man almost killed you. We were watching everything and it was your chef that put poisonous leaves in your mixture. Not someone else's. Yours." He swallowed back the bile and continued pulling her closer. "If I hadn't been there, you could have been the next victim. Get that?"

Hannah pushed him away from her. "Get away from me," she whispered as the doors of the elevator whooshed open, and she rushed out. He gritted his teeth as she ran through the building's front doors. His heart pounded harder than his head, and he clenched his fists.

Damn it all to hell. He stomped to the stairs and bounded back to his office in time to hear his phone ringing. He snatched it up and punched the button.

"Garrett," he bit out.

"Neil, dear, it's Jacqueline. Did I call at a bad

time?"

Neil plopped in his chair and leaned back closing his eyes. "No, ma'am. What can I do for you?" he asked rolling his neck.

"My cousin and I have been doing some talking. She's got a live-in nurse and a large house. Her kids come to visit, but not often, and she's getting lonely. I've agreed to move in with her."

Neil straightened. "Does she live close enough to your doctors'?"

"Oh, yes, and like I said, she's got that nurse of hers. She's a nice young girl."

"What about your furniture and belongings? You need me to get a truck and haul them over there?"

Ms. Jacquie laughed before continuing, "No dear, Lynnette is having her sons do all that for me. Her driver will bring me home and help me gather anything else I need to settle in for now."

Neil frowned. "Well, okay. If you don't need me for anything then."

"Oh, sweet boy, of course I'll need you to come visit me. In fact, I expect you to see me at least once a month. I'll make your favorite cookies," she said.

"Ms. Jacquie, why not just marry me and move into my new house? I have a full kitchen and everything."

"Don't tempt me, young man," she scolded. "Besides, you have that Hannah girl in your sights now."

Neil sputtered, "Oh, no, it's not like that."

"Sure, it isn't. Besides, both of our leases are up next month. No sense my staying at that apartment anymore and since they're raising the rents, it'll be best if you relocate to that house of yours as well."

"That's true," he agreed.

"You take care of yourself, now, you hear?"

"Yes, ma'am," he said, before disconnecting.

He shot up and paced the floor. First Hannah pushed him out and now Ms. Jacquie didn't need him anymore. The band tightened on his chest, and his hands clenched. Laughter from outside his office caught his attention. He flicked a glance toward the other cops joking and teasing like they had no worries. *Bullshit.*

He packed up his files and left. He hopped in his car and headed for the apartment. While he took the steps two at a time, he studied the walls of the apartment building and floor. Worn out carpet and faded paint met him along the way. Time to get out of here. Ms. Jacquie had the precise idea. Once he entered his place, he paused and surveyed the tiny living area. It'd been sufficient before when all he needed was a place to eat and sleep. Devoid of decorations, the apartment carried no semblance of ownership nor personality.

His house sustained personality in the truck loads, even during remodeling. How'd he miss this? Neil sighed and strode into his bedroom, pulled out an overnight bag, an extra-large duffle bag, and his box of old files. He grabbed clothes and stuffed as much as he could in the duffle bag, then carried the box to the kitchen and filled it completely with the paperwork he'd kept in that room. His phone rang, and he tugged it from his pocket, while he entered his bathroom and packed the rest of his personal items.

"Garrett," he answered.

"Super pissed made your woman sparkle. I got

kinda excited," Cast teased.

"Don't go there," Neil warned.

"Got it. So, how'd it go?"

"You calling to gossip?"

"Just wanting to see how bad my partner got scorched, is all."

Neil plopped on the couch and sighed. "She doesn't want to see me anymore."

"Ouch."

"She dredged up Tony's case and how I almost screwed up that investigation," he paused, pinching the bridge of his nose. "I don't know man, she's got me double checking my work."

"No shit?" Cast asked incredulously.

"What?"

"You're hooked if you're letting her dent your confidence man. Tony may not have been guilty of murder, but he sure as hell was running illegal goods."

"Yeah," Neil agreed, and stood. "Listen, I'm clearing out my personals from the apartment tonight. Gonna relocate permanently to the Hanson House."

"What about your furniture and things? Want me to get a team together to grab the rest? It'll just cost you pizza and beer," Cast offered.

"Thanks, but no thanks. I got it arranged already."

"Yeah? Who?"

"You my mother or something?"

"Nope, partner. Stop being an ass. I'm not the one causing you heartache."

Neil paused while opening a bathroom drawer. His stomach tightened into a tight ball. *Heartache? Ah hell.*

"Garrett? You there?"

Neil rolled his shoulders and responded, "Yeah. I

got Buck and his buddies helping me out," he said filling the small shaving kit bag and dumping it in the overnight bag.

"Buck? The C.I. you had last year? Think that's a good idea?"

"He's been on the straight and narrow since then. He's not working as an informant anymore since he knocked up his old lady. They had a baby last month."

"So, they had a baby. Doesn't mean he won't go back. Old habits die hard, especially now he's got another mouth to feed."

Neil carried his bags through the living room and set them near the front door. Switching the phone to the other ear, he dragged the trashcan close to the fridge.

"I've been keeping tabs on him. He's working construction and doing side jobs I find him," he said, while grabbing items out of the fridge and dumping them in the trash.

"You find? You've gotten soft, old man."

"Bite me."

"And you trust him with your stuff?" Cast asked.

"I do. Plus, I'm getting a deal," he paused and sniffed an open container of milk. He jerked back and shuddered. *Spoiled.* "His wife's offered to do the final cleaning of the apartment for me too."

"I don't know, man."

Neil straightened. "Exactly. You don't know." He tied up the trash and dragged the bag out the front door. Spinning around, he searched the apartment confirming he'd gotten all he needed. "Listen, I'm done here and heading back to the house. You got anything else you need to check, Mom?"

"Kiss off," Cast said.

"Yeah, smooches back at you. See you later," Neil retorted, and ended the call. He placed his hands on his waist and surveyed the place he'd called home for the last ten years. *Good riddance.*

After placing the trash in the dumpster and loading his car, he sat quietly behind the wheel and replayed his conversation with Cast. Heartache. He rubbed a palm over his chest. He gasped. *Cookies. Crap.* He hopped out of the car and ran back to the apartment. Shoving open the door he strode over the vinyl flooring and grabbed the small flower decorated tin, Ms. Jacquie had given him, from the counter.

Popping the lid, he peered inside. Six complete cookies nestled among broken pieces and crumbs. He grinned while scooping up crumbs and popped them in his mouth. The flavor of stale oatmeal and sweet cranberry coated his tongue. He munched while locking up and loping down the stairs to his car. *Fortification at its finest.*

****

Once in the driveway of Hanson House, Neil cut the engine and studied the worn siding, cracked windows, and missing shutters. Night had fallen, and the street lamps set a white spray of light across the neighborhood. The paint faded on one side of the house and flat out chipped away on another revealing an ugly brown color underneath. He sighed then opened the door, leaned back against his car, and scanned the land surrounding his house. Splotches of dirt intermingled with green patches of grass. Overgrown hedges poked limbs out like a bush gone wild, clawing its limbs away from the ball of dead branches wrapped around the base. The wind picked up and tossed his hair along with the leaves.

A car passed, and Neil's gaze followed the vehicle up the curved road. Hanson House came into view, and he pulled in the drive and parked. He sighed and pushed away from his car, shutting the door, and sauntered inside his sickly-looking home. *My sickly home*. Time and hard work would make her beautiful again. A lot of solid work and time which he'd have plenty of now. He tossed his papers on the counter and flung open the fridge. He grabbed a beer, popped the lid, and let the cold liquid wet his throat.

"Will you be moping around here this evening?" Muriel asked.

Neil twitched and closed his eyes. "Will you stop sneaking up on me?"

"I say, I do not sneak," she snipped, and her perfume wafted by when her voice neared, "I thought to visit you a bit tonight."

"I don't want to visit," he punctuated each word with a step away from her voice. The room cooled when her shadow followed him. He pivoted and glared. "I don't want company."

"Rudeness is unbecoming a gentleman, you poor thing."

"Stop it. I'm serious," he ordered.

"And if I don't? Have you not realized it's not wise to upset a ghost? Nor would it be wise to work on my home while you're in such a terrible mood. Mistakes happen when one cannot concentrate on the job at hand."

Neil slammed down his beer. "And just what the hell is that supposed to mean? You think I'm making mistakes too?" he demanded.

"Well, I never," Muriel declared.

"I bet you have, lady. Listen, tonight is not a good night to pick a fight with me, whatever you are. I know what I'm doing and if you don't like it, leave." He pinched the bridge of his nose.

"I advised you when you arrived, I have no intention of leaving my home. Watch your language, young man. You do realize anger is a secondary emotion? I read that in an article in Ladies Home Journal. If you can set aside your anger and determine what exactly is causing it, you increase your chances of addressing issues. I'm willing to help you," she offered.

Neil blew out a breath. Stubborn lady. He faced the white shadow who now billowed in front of him. "I have had a really sh—bad day. I am tired and not in any mood to argue, discuss, or rationalize anything. I want…no, need to be alone," he said, and grabbed his beer along with the cookie tin. He strode to the stairs, mounted a couple, and called over his shoulder, "Remember you promised not to go upstairs after that last time. You'll keep that promise now, won't you?"

"I keep my word," Muriel sputtered.

"Good," he mumbled and shot up the remaining steps to the second floor. Heading into his room, he settled in bed and took a slug of his beer while prying open the cookie tin. It's going to be more than crumbs tonight. He set the canister on the side table and studied the full cookie pinched in his fingers. Just one. He tipped his beer and took another swallow while the fizz of the carbonation tingled his tongue.

Taking a small bite of the cookie, he leaned his head back, and closed his eyes savoring the cranberry flavor of his treat. Would Ms. Jacquie be willing to share this recipe? Not that he could bake cookies, but Hannah could. *Hannah.* He frowned while munching another bite of cookie.

Heartache. Flashes of their argument filtered through his mind, and his chest tightened again. His stomach burned, and he pressed a hand against his gut. His heart tripped when an image formed in his mind of Hannah in the kitchen below, baking the oatmeal cranberry cookies. Warm, soft cookies. Warm, soft Hannah. He washed down the bite and set everything aside. Scooting down to sprawl on his back, he stared into the darkness. *Is this how love worked?*

Chapter Nineteen

The morning sun pierced through Neil's eyelids, and he rolled over and burrowed under his pillow. His head throbbed like a jackhammer hitting concrete. *Damn it.* He crawled out of bed and shuffled to the shower—letting the hot water spray over his head and down his back. The pounding receded slightly. Once out and dried off, he checked for any response to his message about taking today off. Cast would understand why he needed a three-day weekend. Maybe. Casts voice confirmed receipt and didn't ask questions. Good.

After dressing, he slugged down a cup of coffee and aspirin. Time to work and stop thinking. A few hours later, his doorbell rang and Neil tossed the rag he'd been using to polish the recently installed wood furniture. Must be the Woo-woo lady Julien told him about. She'd left him a message asking to come on Friday instead of Saturday, as well as explaining the so-called gift. How the hell did anyone expect him to escort this wacko around his house when he didn't actually believe in what she did? But, a gift is a gift, and Julien had talents no one could explain. He wasn't going to argue.

When he opened the door, he did a cursory scan of the woman standing on his porch. Five-four at the most, short tight curly black hair, and if he were into bosomy brunettes wearing long black dresses, hot. Before he could speak, she gave him a big smile and shook his hand.

"Hello there! Thank you so much for allowing me to come into your home. My name is Kim."

She took a step, and Neil scooted back before he could get trampled by the bubbly woman in her quick entrance into the house.

"Julien said you'd recently received the house. It's a pretty home," she said, while she waited for him to catch up. Once behind her, she skipped inside and spun around waving her arms, jingling a large basket over one shoulder, and fanning the air with a folder she clasped in the other.

"Lovely," she twittered, tilting her head back and closing her eyes for a moment before chuckling, then whirling around, and pointing at him, "You're a handsome fellow. All tall, dark, and strong. You work out?"

Neil's face heated, and he rubbed the back of his neck.

"I'm married, not dead," she whispered and winked at him. She chuckled while standing in front of him.

"Let's go into the kitchen as the rest of the house isn't set up for guests just yet," Neil said, then spun around beating a retreat. The clicking of her heels behind him confirmed she followed. He spoke over his shoulder, "Can I get you something to drink? I have water or tea."

"Oh, no thank you. If I drink anymore water, I'll be taking too many breaks from the cleansing," Kim responded. She spun around slowly in the kitchen, before nodding at him. "So beautiful in here. You've done a wonderful job!"

Neil glanced at the cabinets, then the patched wall and frowned. The double stainless steel sink glinted in the light. *Huh.* He shrugged and shifted his stance when Kim opened the pantry door.

"Empty, but it'll fill soon," she mumbled.

"What?" Neil asked.

She waved over her shoulder toward the folder she'd set on the counter, "That's your folder, and I'll go through it in a moment."

Neil glanced at the folder before opening it. Three sheets of paper sat in the side slot. He pulled them out, laid them beside each other, and started reading. She sidled next to him. Close. He shifted his gaze and peered at her.

Kim's eyes twinkled, and she grinned and nudged his ribs. She pointed to the first one.

"This explains why cleansing is important when you first buy a new home, as well as how often it is needed. Think of it like a spiritual spring cleaning. Clear out the negative and invite the positive energies," she paused, glanced over his shoulder, and returned her gaze to him. "I'll talk as I walk so you'll know what I'm doing. I will be chanting in whispers. You may not understand what I'm saying. However, remember I mean you no harm and I'm here to help."

She pointed to the second page which listed herbs and incense. "These are incense and herbs you can use around the house to help the energy. Sage is good for clearing and lemon grass is good for bringing in positive energy. Never use both at the same time," she paused and tapped his arm. "It's best not to overlap."

Neil tipped his head. *No clue.*

"We'll start outside to be sure you have no worries

regarding the land here. I did some research," she paused and planted her hands on her hips while spinning around and facing the kitchen. "I see you," she said to the empty room. "Yes, I understand." She lifted a hand and wiggled her fingers before turning back to Neil. "Your friend was worried I'd try to push her out."

Neil stilled and kept his face blank. "Friend?" he asked.

Kim pursed her lips, and her gaze swept across his face. "We'll talked about that later." She picked items from her bag and held up a large string wrapped item.

"That looks like a large joint." Neil scowled.

"It's not. It's sage. I'm going to light it and walk around. You're not allergic to any herbs or plants, are you? Not that I carry anything that could be considered bane."

"Bane?" Neil asked.

"Poison…well, used in its archaic form. Modern definition is more like a pest or irritant," she added, and leaned in. "Bane of my existence, for example."

Neil nodded, "I've heard of that."

"Before I light and cleanse, I want to walk everywhere and measure the energy. You're welcome to join me. I love the company of a sexy man."

Neil coughed, and Kim giggled tugging on his shirt.

"Come, I don't bite…well…not during a cleansing anyway."

He bit the inside of his cheek. *Great.*

Kim scooted to the front door, and Neil followed.

"The energy out here is incredibly good," Kim announced as she skirted the corner, and nearly skipped toward the side yard. She pointed at the storage building sitting off the back corner of the property. "Do you use that? We'll need to go in there as well."

The sun peeked from between clouds and glanced off her head revealing a purple tinge. *Purple?* Neil trotted up behind her when she slid the doors open and prepared to step inside. He clasped her elbow. "I haven't been able to stabilize this building and for safety reasons, I can't let you go inside."

"Oh, that's fine. I'll stand here outside the door then." Her chirpy voice echoed into the half empty building as she peered inside. She lifted her hands, palms up in front of her. What was she doing? Feeling the air? Neil stopped short of laughing out loud and waited. *Patience.*

Kim murmured words too low for him to catch, then nodded and walked away. A breeze made her scarves of various bright colors dance in her wake. Neil frowned then peeked inside the shed, noticing nothing but the dusty web-covered interior. He shrugged and pivoted to discover the woman had passed through his backyard and was almost around the other side of the house. Damn, she was fast. He rushed to catch up to her as she stepped onto his front porch. Without speaking, she opened the door and traipsed inside.

He followed. Like he had a choice? He glanced at the clock. How long would this take? Was he doomed to follow this lady for hours or less? Could he ask without offending her? *Damn.* Kim now had a large bell in one hand and paused to adjust the ribbon.

"It's going to get loud now. I'm going to go room to room while ringing this bell. It will stir up and shift the energy around, so it's not stagnate," she said with a grin. "Again, you're more than welcome to follow me around, if you wish. In fact," she paused and chuckled, "I recommend it in case you have any questions."

"Every room?" Neil asked.

"Yes, we must. It's the best way to do this properly," Kim responded.

"Okay, I'll follow to make sure you don't trip on anything. I hope Julien explained I'm in the early stages of renovation. The kitchen and the bedrooms are my main points of operations for now."

"It's fine. I've worked homes in worst conditions. I'll watch where I step."

****

Two hours later, Neil sat with Kim at his kitchen island sipping tea. She'd mentally worn him out traipsing around his yard and house, chattering away. The aroma of sage permeated his clothes and filled his nostrils. Not a bad smell, but as soon as she left, he'd be opening more windows than she had.

After taking a small sip of her tea, Kim slipped off the chair and rounded the island. Her back faced him while she ran her fingertips around the sink and along the counter tops. She paused and beamed at him.

"Please get that book off the top of your cabinet here," she requested while pointing to the tall cabinet on his right.

He frowned. He'd checked that space the day he moved in and found nothing. He blew out a breath, stood and stretched upward. His fingers bumped an object, and his jaw slackened. Lifting on the tips of his toes, he searched farther back and clasped the edge of a book. Tugging it to the edge, he tightened his grip and dropped down to hand it to Kim.

He stared at the worn edges of the spine and

yellowed pages of the book while she opened and flipped through it. What the hell?

"It's a cookbook," Kim said then flipped to the front of the book. Peering closer at the typesetting, she whispered, "Published in 1946." She glanced at him. "Recognize it?"

"No. In fact," he paused scanning the tops of the cabinets, "I checked those spaces, and they were empty the day I moved in."

Kim twittered and placed the book on the counter. She clasped her hands together and took a deep breath before continuing, "How long have you known of Muriel's existence here?"

Neil remained silent.

Her lips lifted on one side, and she shook her head, causing her curls to bounce.

She wasn't budging. Great. Neil coughed and returned to his seat staring at his hands.

"Since I moved in," he mumbled.

"You understand she's bound herself to this house and has no intention of ever leaving, correct?"

He lifted his head to stare at Kim. "You can't make her leave? I thought that's one of the things you did…or assumed you did. I don't get all this mumbo jumbo sh…stuff."

Kim giggled and patted his hand. "It's okay. Most people don't understand, nor want to understand." She tapped her fingers on the book. "Muriel is not a spiteful spirit. I believe she has chosen to stay here in order to continue the hospitality she worked so hard to obtain during the time she lived here."

"She's a busybody," Neil countered.

"Perhaps. If you can understand she means no

harm and that sometimes, spirits understand things we, the living, can't…or refuse to understand."

"So?"

"Besides, I've already told her I wouldn't make her leave. I can, however, give you names of other mediums that can help clear her out, if you absolutely believe it's necessary. I'd like you to think hard on it first," she paused and padded her hair then winked at him. "Sometimes, a resident spirit can be very helpful."

Conversations he'd had with Muriel flashed through his mind. She'd been more a nuisance than mean. Would it hurt her to leave?

"Do they feel…pain?" He'd never hurt a woman on purpose…even a ghost.

"Pain?"

"If I choose to have her cleared out. Would it hurt her?"

"They have no physical sensation, if that is what you're asking." She placed a hand on his arm and gave it a little squeeze.

He nodded at Kim then cleared his throat.

"I'll think about it."

Kim clapped her hands and grinned wide. "Good." She pulled out a tall white candle in a clear glass vase. She placed it near his sink and lit it while whispering a chant. She returned to her seat and nudged him pointing at the candle, "Let that burn out. Don't blow it out."

"Why?" Neil asked.

She glanced at her watch before responding, "It's necessary to let it burn out on its own. I'm running out of time, and I have a message for you," she said softly.

"Message? From Muriel?" There, he no longer was able to pretend she didn't exist.

"No, not from her. From one of my own guides. They said to tell you, there is another spirit who is very lost and confused attached to a loved one of yours. This spirit died suddenly and is having problems moving on. Do you understand?"

Hannah's face appeared in his mind. "I'm not sure, but I think so."

"You will be asked to help with this spirit's endeavors. You must keep an open mind and answer with your heart," she said and leaned in to drop a quick peck on his cheek. Her breath tickled his ear when she whispered, "Your decision will strongly impact your relationship with this loved one. It could end it."

Neil jerked back and glared at her. *What the hell?* Prickly pins poked his spine, and he shuddered clasping Kim's shoulder.

"Who is the loved one? I need to know for sure," he demanded.

Kim dipped to release herself and whipped around grabbing her basket and belongings.

"I'm sorry, I don't have any more information. I need to go now. I'm late. You have my card. Please call with anything else you might need," she said and rushed out of the house.

He froze unable to follow her. His chest squeezed like a large hand cuff had been placed on him and tightened. His breath caught in his lungs, and he swallowed past the lump in his throat. Black specks swam before his vision. He dropped his head into his hands and gasped for air. End? Hannah? Sure, she was pissed at him. But, she'd be fine once she cooled off...right? Had he fooled himself into believing they had more?

He jolted up and pounded his fist on the island. *Oh hell no.* He grabbed his phone and punched in Hannah's number.

Chapter Twenty

Hannah tightened the scarf around her neck, and after locking her car, ran inside the school building. The lingering aromas of baking were missing and replaced with stringent cleaning odors. Frowning, she dropped her head and rushed toward the instructor's offices. She moved silently from one door to the next until she located the one with Chef Caulder's nameplate. She swiped the access card she'd kept, and the knob twisted easily, and the click echoed in the empty hall.

She slipped inside and glanced around. The hall light peeked through the open door and cast a pale light on the desk, chair, and surrounding bookcases. She closed the door, pitching the office into complete darkness. After pulling out the pocket flashlight she'd tucked away earlier, she flashed the beam toward his desk.

Hannah maneuvered around two metal chairs and gasped when her hip nudged a side table containing cutting knives. She grabbed two before they fell and sighed her when the plastic sheaths kept the noise muffled. After replacing them, she slid in Chef's chair and frowned at the mountain of papers sitting in the middle of his desk. How the heck am I going to find anything here?

She slumped, then leaned back in the chair. The movement caused the hinges to screech out. *Shoot.* She jerked back to an upright position, and tucking the flashlight in between her lips, pulled open the front desk drawer. Pens, pencils, and sticky notes filled the cavity. She glanced through the notes. Class information. Hannah pushed it shut and pulled open the side drawer. A thick black journal sat under more pens, measuring spoons, and two additional knives. She lifted it, opened to a random page and read the words written inside.

Dr. Sullivan has pressed me more sternly to take charge in order to get past Betty's death. It's not so much to get over her that I need now… I've found Hilly, and I know what I must do for us to be together again. I must show her I can help her fulfill her dream. I will take charge as the doctor ordered. I will make her dream come true. Then she will see how much I truly love her. How much we were meant to be together.

Hannah gasped, while her stomach clenched, and she dropped the journal. Her hand covered her mouth, and she tightly squeezed her eyes shut. Oh, no. Chef. She opened her eyes, picked up the journal again, and flipped to the last page.

Today is the day. One more contender to remove and the win will be there for the taking. My love has so much more talent than I ever knew. She is a natural. I should have remembered how quickly she learned. I find there are many things from the past I am forgetting. With each visit, Dr. Sullivan has now increased the length of times of my hypnotherapy sessions. I admit I feel stronger after each visit, even though I feel as though I am losing something else. But I can't put my finger on it. There are memories that flash for a second, and before I can grab and hold onto them, they fade. As I dressed this morning, I found a photo of my wedding day. It took over an hour of staring before I realized I couldn't remember my own wife's name.

No matter. I'll see Hilly today and her smile will make everything fade in the background, as always. My heart beats stronger now. Soon. Soon we will be together.

Hannah flipped the pages looking for the date of Anita's accident. Chef noted the dates in tenths. She peered closer. Tenth, twentieth, thirtieth. Great. She searched her memory. Anita passed away before the tenth. Starting on that page, she quickly scanned the words written on the page. The writing started to get shaky and became stronger toward the end. She frowned then gasped, when she discovered Anita's name written and circled in the journal.

Blowing out a breath, she read the passage carefully. She closed and returned the journal to the drawer. The police had yet to clear out Chef's office. Hannah cleared the area so the journal sat on top and would be the first thing anyone discovered when the drawer was opened. She paused and searched the office. Finding a cloth, she carefully wiped the journal keeping her fingers away from the surface. She shrugged. Unlikely anyone would try to dust for fingerprints. But the movies always showed some idiot forgetting to clean their fingerprints and getting in trouble. No way would she let that happen.

Hannah rose and after wiping every surface she had touched coming in, closed the door, and paused in the hall. No noise. Not even security? She shook her head and headed out. Neil needed to know about the notebook and its contents. The scene of their argument flooded her mind. Her chest tightened at the words they'd thrown at each other. Would he even listen to her now? Should she try?

She got in her car and cranked up the heat. Perhaps it would be smarter to find out who was going to defend Chef Caulder and call them? *No.* She trusted Neil even though he was such a jerk. Her phone rang, and she jumped glancing at the display. *Rose.*

****

Neil tugged at the tie that kept trying to strangle him. Blasted suits. He checked his phone again. Blasted phones. He strode into the courthouse, flashing his badge at the guard, and got the clearance he needed. He worked his way through people meandering and stopping to check when and where their case hearings would be scheduled. He ignored them and beelined it to the elevators, catching one before the doors slid shut.

Slipping inside, he punched the button for the sixth floor and tapped his foot. He slid a sideways glance over the occupants. Eight civilians, various social levels noted by their clothing, nothing odd. *Good.* He switched to stare at the light above and each floor dinged its arrival. Why did people do this? Boredom? He let his mind go back to his argument with his woman. Four days ago. Four long days and nights. Damn, even pissed off, she excited him.

At least she'd returned his call. Even though he'd missed it, he'd received her voice mail. Apparently, she'd gone where she shouldn't and found the killer's journal. The poor sap chef had fallen hard for her mother and mistaken Hannah for the woman. How bad had his grief been, that he'd allowed some wacko shrink to convince him killing was okay?

Hannah hadn't been the target. He frowned when the replay of their recording that day filtered through his mind. He missed her moving her pot. If Patterson hadn't caught Caulder dropping poisonous rhubarb leaves in the other students' pot, he might have gotten away with it. His heart pounded when the memory of that moment flashed in. He'd thought it was meant for Hannah. He'd almost drawn his gun. Damn, that would not have been good.

Her face pictured in his mind. She'd be the death of him. He grinned. Yeah, it'd be one hell of a death, though. That voice of hers acted like a siren in the ocean. His mind could be clear, but his body responded the instant her voice touched him. Even during their fight, her sweet scent called to him.

Images of her lying in his bed, her kisses, the sparks in her eyes when she argued with him…the fire in those same eyes when they made love. He shifted his weight. *Down boy.* The woman standing next to him cleared her throat, and Neil glanced at her. Long haired brunette, slim, model worthy. Too skinny. She smiled at him and batted her lashes. Nothing. Neil lifted one side of his mouth in a half smile and resumed staring at the floor indicator lights. The woman sniffed and took two steps away from him.

When the eighth floor arrived, the doors opened, and Neil strode out, heading down toward the meeting room that had been reserved. After a quick knock, he opened the door. The prosecutor waved him in.

"Hey, Russ, thanks for meeting with me this morning," he said, while shaking his friend's hand.

"Anytime." Russ glanced at his watch. "I have a

few minutes before the judge returns. What do you need?"

"What's your position on the Caulder case?"

"Funny you should ask." The attorney flipped open one of the files on the table before him. "I received a message from my assistant saying there was a journal found in evidence taken from the chef's school office indicating the man had issues."

"Yeah. That's what I heard. He's unbalanced. You looking to ask for prison time?"

Russ frowned then answered, "He's killed and incapacitated innocent folks. You don't think he deserves it?"

"That's not what I'm saying," Neil said, then cleared his throat. "Look, all I'm saying is that if defense pulls the insanity card…I might not mind it so much in this case."

"What? Who are you and what have you done with my friend Neil?"

"Ha ha. Look, Russ. I'm going to call in my favor you owe me and ask that you don't dismiss the chance for this guy to be locked up in a hospital. If it's for the rest of his life, I'm okay with it."

Russ sat and flipped through the rest of the papers in the folder. He flipped it shut and stood. "I don't have a problem with that. Defense has already asked and received a psych evaluation clearance before the hearing. I'd like to know why though. We've worked together for far too long to not have an explanation on why you'd be okay with any kind of diminished capacity defense."

Neil shrugged and leaned back against the door but kept silent.

"I'll let you get away with this for now, because I have less than a minute to get back to court." Russ nudged Neil aside. "I'll catch up with you later."

Neil grabbed his arm. "Thanks."

"Yep."

After he left, Neil took several breaths and popped his neck. The tension eased somewhat, and he unclenched his jaw. That was a conversation that would be a long time off. He had other things to worry about.

He swung open the door and aimed for the stairs. No elevator this time. He loped down the steps, while ideas flickered in and out of his head. He had to find a way to get Hannah back in his life. Hell, get her back and keep her there. After having nearly daily contact for the last month, this last week's silence about killed him. The kitchen's final touches were being done today, and the items Muriel suggested arrived last night. Yep, he'd listen to the ghost, but his woman would not be able to resist the gadgets and machines a chef would drool over. If she did resist, he was screwed. He had no idea what half those fancy things did. They sure looked sharp on the counters though.

He arrived at his car and climbed in. After checking to make sure he had the decorating magazine with him, Neil cranked the engine. Time to set things in motion.

Chapter Twenty-One

Saturday morning, Neil folded the new kitchen towels and looped them through the double oven's handle, then stepped back to admire the shiny chrome.

"Ah, sure looks nice. That young lady of yours will adore this. Smart move getting this all set up early. You do intend to propose, yes? No fallen woman is going to be staying in Hanson house."

Neil slid a glance toward Muriel's white form. He blinked, closed his eyes, counted to ten, and then reopened his lids. Yep, still there.

"Oh, bless your heart. You truly believe that I'm a figment of your imagination after all this time? Didn't anything that psychic woman say stick in your head?" Her form shifted, and she moved toward the window. A breeze ruffled the curtains. "I say, how can you be so good at your job if you can't remember anything as simple as a resident ghost?"

"Just because she says you exist doesn't mean you do."

Muriel's laughter tickled his neck. "Truly?"

Neil planted his hands on his hips. "Fine. You exist. Happy?"

"I will once I hear the words 'I do' come out of that beautiful girl's mouth."

"Listen, I'll propose when I'm ready and not before. I'll survive with you living here, but there's

going to be rules. Rule one—" he held up a finger—
"you are never to go upstairs without permission. Rule
two—" Neil raised a second finger—"No dictating how
I live my life."

"Well, I declare."

"Well, you can do all the declaring you want. But I
will do what I want, when I want," he said.

"Do you want to marry her?"

Neil's heart palpated then a warmth flushed over
his skin. "Yes," he whispered.

"She is terribly close to her family," Muriel said.

"I know and that's good with me."

"She'll expect to meet any living family you have."
Neil growled. "No dictating."

"I'm not, sweetie. I'm simply wondering how long
it's been, since you've spoken to your own mother?
How long do you intend to punish her for seeking her
own happiness? Was it selfish? Perhaps. Yet, it's hard
to move forward if you still have a past you're fighting.
Don't you agree?"

"You expect me to make up with my mother?"

"Reach out to her. Give her the opportunity to
apologize? Lord knows everyone changes with time."

"I don't know if I can do that…or want to do that."

"Perhaps your woman will help you," she
suggested.

"I don't know. I have a bunch of things I need to
get done," he paused, and took a deep breath before
continuing, "I'm going to see if I can get Hannah over
here next weekend after the initial court hearing. When
I do, will you not be here? One thing at a time, okay?"

"Yes, sweetie… I'll be invisible."

"No, not invisible. I want to be alone with her. Go

up to the attic or somewhere."

"But, you told me not to go upstairs."

Neil stepped toward the ghostly shape and pointed his finger. "You know what I mean."

Muriel chuckled and began fading. Once she vanished, he stood alone.

****

Sunday morning Neil jumped out of bed and rushed into the shower. Ideas of how to get his stubborn woman to see his point of view and understand why he did what he did ruffled through his head. *Blast it.* It'd been a week since their fight. The image of her face at the hearing when she discovered a deal had been made with the prosecutor etched in his mind. His pulse picked up when he rinsed and dried off. Honesty. Blunt truth. That was the best way to do this. Any other way fell way short.

He dressed and made toast in the fancy four-slotted machine made for bagels and such. When he spread peanut butter across the bread, a hum floated across the room. Muriel's shimmering shape solidified while she sat at the counter island.

"Today is the day?" she asked.

"Yep," he responded.

"Nervous?"

"Hell, no," Neil lied, while trying to swallow down a bite of toast in a suddenly dry throat.

"You wouldn't be normal if you weren't at least a little bit nervous, honey."

"I'm fine," he said around another bite of toast. He choked and grabbed a glass of water to wash it down. Screw this. He tossed the rest in the trash and glared at Muriel.

"Remember what I said last week."

"I will, sugar," she said. "The Daughters of the Magnolia would be proud of you. Oh dear, I'm proud of you." She sniffled.

Oh no. No tears. Even ghost tears. His hands shook, and he scanned the room looking anywhere except at the ghostly woman crying softly in his kitchen.

"Please stop crying," he begged.

"It's happy tears, honey," she responded then waved her hand. "I'll be fine. Go on and get her."

Neil sighed. Women.

He took off and got in his car then he checked the clock. He'd be at Hannah's place in less than an hour. He had one hour to figure out how he could convince her to come to his house and see what he'd done—with her in mind. All the new gadgets, shiny floors, everything. He shifted in the seat. The picture of the small box sitting on his dresser popped in his mind. His heart rate kicked up a notch. One step at a time.

Neil arrived at the apartment building and noted Tony helping a woman around Hannah's age carry a chair up the stairs to Hannah's apartment. What's that about? He scanned the parking lot. No other activity except those two.

He parked and took the stairs two at a time, reaching the door when Tony exited.

"Whoa dude," Tony said. "What's the hurry?"

Neil tipped his head and peered around Tony into the apartment then back at Tony.

"Where's Hannah?"

Tony's face flushed a dark red, and he bit his lip. "Um, I thought we couldn't be making contact being as

I'm a felon and you're a cop."

Neil advanced until the toes of his boots hit Tony's tennis shoes. "Where is she?"

The woman Tony had helped appeared.

"Excuse me, you need to back away now. I am dialing 9-1-1. See me dialing it?" she said.

"Andrea, it's okay," Tony said. "I know him. Besides, he's a cop."

Andrea lifted her chin and stared. "And you are?"

Neil coughed and stepped back. Tony shifted, and Andrea moved alongside him, "Tony?" she asked placing her hand on his shoulder.

"Andrea, this is Neil Garrett. Someone Aunt Hannah knows," he explained.

"What's going on?" Neil asked Tony.

"Rude, aren't you?" Andrea questioned and her posture straightened.

Neil glanced down and noted her hands clenching in a spasm. *Damn it.* He sighed and plastered a smile on his face. "I'm looking for Hannah. We had a disagreement, and I'm needing to talk to her." Tony already told her who he was.

Andrea's head bobbed, and she moved her hands behind her. "She's meeting with her cousin Michael about that job in New York."

Tony gasped, and Neil shot him a frown.

"What job?"

"Um, perhaps you should call her," Andrea suggested, stepping back.

Neil pointed a finger at Tony. "Talk."

"Mr. Garrett, really."

"No, it's okay, Andrea. He's cool when he's not pissed." He winked at Andrea before continuing, "I'll be right back, and we'll get the rest of your things carried up, okay?"

Andrea remained silent, but smiled.

Neil followed Tony a few feet away. They both leaned against the railing and regarded the half empty parking lot. His stomach clenched, and he gripped the rail so tightly his knuckles whitened.

"Tell me," he ordered.

"Michael owns a restaurant in New York. He's been pressuring Hannah to relocate up there and help him expand his bakery department. Since the competition was cancelled, Hannah won't have the money to open her own place. I think this might be her one chance of at least running a bakery. Michael's promised her full rein in doing whatever she wants."

Fuck. Neil swallowed past the lump in his throat. "Is she seriously considering the offer?"

Tony shrugged. "Who knows, man. I hope not. I don't want her to move away."

"She's meeting with him now?" Maybe he could stop her.

"Huh? Oh, no. She drove to her parents' house to talk to Gramps first. Then she'll be coming back to meet him for dinner." Tony pushed away from the rail and grabbed Neil's shirt. "You're not going to let her go, are you?"

Neil searched the boy's face. Hope.

"Not if I have anything to say about it," Neil stated.

Tony laughed.

"Whatever she decides, she said after dinner, she'd be heading back up to spend the rest of the weekend with Grams."

Neil stared at the ground. No way to get her

tonight. He'd have to try tomorrow. He laid a hand on Tony's shoulder. "I hear you got free of the leg shackle."

Tony grinned. "Yep. I'm on stock duty at the food bank. Long as I clock in, Officer Dickhead said he'd only see me once a month."

"Dude, show him some respect."

"Not happening. Good luck with Hannah," Tony said and walked away.

Neil watch him until he entered the apartment. He made his way back to his car and ran his fingers through his hair. One more night. Could he wait? *Damn.* Not like he had a choice. Besides, Hannah was worth it. He hummed as he started his car and headed back home. At the first stoplight, he watched as a couple holding hands, walked across the street.

Hell no. The light turned green, and he hit the gas heading toward the highway. Patience be damned. He'd waited long enough.

Chapter Twenty-Two

Hannah pushed the porch swing into motion as she sipped from her iced cold tea. The sweetness slipped over her tongue while she gazed at the sky. The temperature had dropped five degrees since she'd first stepped outside—two hours ago. One more hour and she'd need her coat. Her mother patted her leg while the wind blew tendrils of hair across her face.

"I'm so sorry, baby."

"Mom, it's not your fault. He was confused and even more messed up by that psychiatrist. I'm hoping the deal made was Neil's idea," Hannah whispered.

"He seems like he'd do most anything you ask," her mother said, then chuckled.

"Not true. At least, I don't think so." She twisted in the seat and faced her mom. "You should have seen him at the school." Hannah shuddered. "I'd never want to be a criminal around him."

"That bad?"

"Yes. But, it wasn't personal." Hannah frowned. "I wish I'd seen that at the time. I took it all personally. He hasn't tried contacting me, and it's been over a week now."

"When something like this happens, the closer you are to someone, the harder it is to stay objective."

"Well—" Hannah shrugged, before continuing— "since the competition was cancelled, it looks like I'll have to wait for the bakery."

"Honey, you don't have to wait. Your father and I can help you. We want to help you."

"I know. I need to do this on my own," she said.

"And Michael's offer? What about that?"

"I'm undecided."

"Really?" Her mother raised an eyebrow.

"Mom," Hannah began, then stopped when her phone rang. The display said Tony, so she answered, mouthing to her mother his name. Her mom nodded, rose, and returned inside the house.

"Tony, what's up?" Hannah asked.

"Guess who was here looking for you while I was helping Andrea settle in?"

"No clue."

"Come on, guess," Tony teased.

"Tony."

"Yeah, yeah. Neil. He seemed desperate to talk to you."

Hannah's heart tripped, and she gripped the phone tightly. Her palms dampened.

"What did he say?"

"He needed to talk to you," he responded.

"He has my number."

"I don't think it was over the phone. He seemed a bit beat up and nervous. You two fight?" Tony asked.

"Why do you ask that?"

"Because he acted like a boyfriend whose girlfriend is avoiding him. You two got a thing going, I guessed."

"How?"

"Not saying. But listen, I gotta tell you something."

"Tony, he's not as bad as you think." Hannah

pulled the phone away from her ear when Tony's laughter rang out. When he stopped laughing and gasped for breath, she continued, "What's so funny?"

"I was about to say the same thing to you. You know, no matter what my mom and dad says, I wasn't in the wrong place at the wrong time. I was heading down a dead-end road when Neil arrested me. He saved my life. It made me think a lot about what I've done and where I want to go. I found out from my probation officer that even though Neil and I can't see or talk to each other, Neil's been checking up on me and giving the man a mouthful if he doesn't follow through on the rehabilitation opportunities available. I think he's been watching out for me," he paused, "no, I know he's been watching out for me. This has been going on since I got out, so you can't say it's because of you."

"I wasn't going to say that," Hannah said.

"But you were thinking of it. He's a fair man...a bit on the strict side, but fair. I think he'd be the best cop to have on your side if you needed one."

Hannah pressed her lips together and closed her eyes. He spoke the truth. Drat it all. She'd gone and fallen in love with the man.

"You there?" Tony asked.

"I'm here," she whispered.

"Think about it, will you?"

"I will." She rubbed a palm across her forehead.

"Promise?"

"I promise," Hannah answered, then disconnected the call. Well, that was that. She punched in Michael's number and waited for him to answer. When he did, she explained she couldn't accept his offer. She hung up the phone and grinned. She was in love with a Neanderthal.

She laughed and headed inside to find her mother and tell her the news.

****

A loud knock at the front door echoed through the house, when Hannah and her parents sat down for dinner. Her mother rose only to be waved down by her father.

"Sit and eat. I'll check the door," he said, then strode toward the front of the house.

Within minutes he returned with Neil striding behind him.

"Look who's come for dinner," her father announced.

Hannah gasped softly, and her stomach fluttered like a powered whisk in a bowl. She pressed her trembling hand against her thigh before raising her gaze to Neil. His gaze reflected the light from the chandelier, and his mouth bore a grim smile.

"Do you mind?" he asked in a deep voice.

She shook her head and waved at the seat across from her. "Have a seat."

Neil sat and after a moment helped himself to food while carrying on a conversation with her parents about the weather. Great. Weather talk? She popped a chunk of watermelon in her mouth, and ignored the flavor as her mind shuffled ideas. What should she say? How should she act? They needed to talk privately. But, that wasn't going to happen here in the kitchen or near her parents. Later. His woodsy scent carried over the table and wrapped around her. Her body warmed and tingled begging for his touch.

After eating her parents shooed them out to the back porch while they cleaned up. She sat on the swing and waited silently. Would he sit next to her or stand away? She'd told him to stay out of her life. Obviously, he didn't believe it to mean permanently. Thank goodness.

The swing hinges squeaked when Neil squeezed in next to her. She studied him from lowered lashes as he shifted closer and wrapped an arm across the back of her shoulder. She remained still. His foot pushed the swing into motion, and his chest pressed against her side. He sighed, and his hand stroked her hair. She bit the inside of her lip. He'd have to talk first.

"So, Tony told me about Michael's offer," he said in a low voice.

"I know," she said.

"You take it?" Neil asked.

"Would it matter to you if I did?"

****

Neil forced his muscles to relax and inhaled deeply. *Damn.* Wrong move. Her scent wove itself around them. *Yes, desperately.* He cleared his throat and rocked his head to work out the kinks in his neck. Time to man up.

"Yes, it would," he responded.

"Why?"

Why? He had to tell her why now? He had this all planned. She needed to be at his house and see his kitchen…her kitchen to understand. How the hell could he explain this to her? Think, man.

"Because I don't want you to leave Georgia," he answered.

"Why?"

"Is that the only word you know? Why?"

Her eyebrows rose at the crisp tone of his voice.

"Sorry. Listen, I pulled in a favor and the prosecutor agreed to diminished capacity. Your chef won't go to prison. He'll be locked up in a hospital though for the rest of his life. That was the deal. You okay with that?"

"I am," she responded.

Okay, one hurdle done. He leaned in to sniff her hair...damn she smelled so good. She pulled away an inch or two and kept silent. *Crap.*

"I saw you got a new roommate. Where'd you meet her?"

"Through a friend. She's big on running...almost obsessed with it. But she's good. She works as a teaching assistant at Southeast University, in the linguistics department. She's shy."

"She wasn't when I met her," he said tugging a strand of her hair.

"I'd told her about what's been going on recently. She's simply being protective."

"Makes sense," he said, then stopped the swing before continuing, "Hannah, I'd like you to come over to the house. I have something I want to show you."

"Why?"

"What?" Neil asked.

"Why do you want to show me something? I mean, since all I do is see kittens and rainbows and not reality."

"Puppies," he said.

"Puppies?"

"Puppies and rainbows and maybe that's okay. After all this time being on the police force, it's easy to get jaded. When faced with all the bad things people do, it's easy to forget the nice stuff."

"So, you admit I can see reality?"

Neil cleared his throat again. "Yes, you can. You should understand that I can't afford to wear rose colored glasses in my job. If I do, I could get killed."

Hannah shifted and twisted in the seat facing him.

"I never asked you to see the world as I do. I merely asked for you to understand how I see it and why and accept how I am. Just accept me for who I am and what I want and admit that your comment about the money was way off base."

"It was. I'm sorry about that. Really sorry. I know better. The whole situation was wound tighter than a cannon." He leaned in to drop a soft kiss on her cheek. "I do accept you for who you are. I want you as you are."

"You'll have to prove it, Neil," she said.

"Tell me how."

"You need to come with me and help me help Rose," she returned, watching him.

His neck itched. Ghosts, great. *Ah hell.* At least it wasn't breaking the law.

"This is that important to you?" Neil asked.

"It is. It's even more important that you're there. You read the file, so you know more details than I do," she said, and shifted even closer to kiss the edge of his chin. She ran her fingers in his hair. "I talked to Victoria and know everything we need to do."

"When?"

"Tonight."

"Agreed." Negotiation time.

"You'll do this with me?"

Neil snuggled her neck and whispered in her ear, "I'll do this with you if we can make out first. Then when we're all done with Rose, you have to come home with me."

Hannah giggled, grabbed his face, and attacked his mouth. His body rocked with the heat of her fire.

****

That night, Neil swung and parked his car at the curb, under the single lamp, near the entry of the parking lot. The evening's humidity caused a foggy mist to blanket the concrete. No white lines to mark spaces were visible. Scattered leaves from nearby trees hung off the untrimmed back hedge lining the secluded area. Its overgrown limbs poked out a half hazard cage, nearly five feet up the one and only security call post. The blue lighted button barely penetrated the branches to be noticeable. He rolled down his window, turned off the ignition, and surveyed the area. No student should be using this lot. He slowed his breathing and listened. The buzzing of die-hard mosquitoes and crickets hummed their fight against the oncoming winter.

Hannah shifted, and Neil placed a palm on her knee to hold her in place. She was not getting out until he had a chance to scope out the area. It was too late to keep Rose alive, but no one would hurt his woman. *His woman*. He inhaled a deep breath and opened his door. Hannah reached for her door, and he hit the lock button. She stared at him.

"What's wrong?" she whispered, glancing around.

"Nothing is going to happen until I check this place out first," he said.

Hannah let out a breath and pulled out her phone. Glancing down and then around, she spoke, "You have ten minutes before she calls."

"Fine. Keep your butt in that seat while I take a

look…please."

She nodded and leaned back against the seat. The pose pushed her breasts up and curved her back. Neil's body instantly reacted. He bit back a groan and trotted down toward the hedge. Control. He needed to remain in control. He investigated all around the lot, checking behind hedges and posts. Nothing stood out. He returned and nodded to Hannah, pushing the unlock button. Once she joined him, he held her hand.

"Okay, tell me what to do."

"Victoria says we need to clear our minds, wait until she calls and then hopefully, we'll see something."

Neil nodded. "Then what?"

"Well, if I understand correctly, Rose has blocked out her death and skipped onto getting into her car safely. Although she knows she's dead, she hasn't allowed her spirit to experience it. Only by emotionally dying along with her body, can her spirit release…or something like that."

"Sounds harsh."

Hannah shrugged, "Victoria says that's why a lot of spirits are earthbound…they have unrealized emotional experience to complete first. Based on Rose's experience, this is the one thing we could come up with for why she's still here."

"So, we stand here while you talk to her? Why not just talk to her over the phone to help her if the chances of us seeing something is next to nil?" Didn't make sense. Stand in the middle of nowhere to help a ghost go away. *Great.* The guys would have a field day with this if they knew. Then again…it might explain Muriel's problem. Victoria was going to hear from him soon.

The jingling tune echoed, and Hannah gasped. Neil jerked his head toward the direction she faced. A small red compact shimmered in the fog. Neil blinked and squinted. Yep. That's a car. He took a step before Hannah's voice stopped him.

"Rose?"

****

Hannah gasped as the mist of the night gathered tightly to outline the shape of a woman standing near the car.

"Rose?" She whispered again as the white cloud swirled and took form. Hannah's eyes pooled, and she ignored the tears dripping down her cheeks. Her roommate stood in front of her.

"Hannah?"

Hannah bit her lip, swallowed the lump in her throat, and nodded. "It's me, Rose. I'm here like I said I would be to help you." She lifted her hand and met ice cold air after her fingertips touched the area of Rose's shoulder. She dropped her arm and tipped her chin in the direction of the vehicle across the lot.

"That's your car. And this is Neil, he'll go with us." Hannah pointed at Neil who stood stock still.

"It's already different, Hannah. We're not repeating our regular conversation."

"This should work," Hannah paused and cleared her throat before going on, "remember that night, Rose. You have to remember the walk to your car."

The vision of Rose moved like a slow breeze, floating inches above the ground toward the car. Neil grabbed Hannah's hand, and they walked behind the spirit. Hannah leaned toward him and whispered, "Do you see her?"

At Neil's nod, she sighed. What a relief he could see her too. When they got a few feet from her car, Rose's form shifted and swirled like a small bush rustled by the wind.

"Rose," Hannah spoke softly. "Remember I'm right here with you. You're not alone."

"I truly think there needs to be an emergency post out here."

"Rose, you're not on the phone with me. Remember, I didn't answer that night. Maybe you thought that as you walked?"

"I did. I was thinking of that exact thing when you didn't answer," Rose said, when the wind around all three of them kicked up.

Fallen leaves jostled each other in their race across the asphalt. Hannah shivered but continued following Rose.

"I unlocked the car," Rose said, and a beep echoed sharply.

Neil squeezed Hannah's hand when she jumped from the noise.

"A noise sounded behind me. I dropped my keys when I turned around," Rose said, and her form solidified for a second showing her face clearly. Her eyes went wide, and her mouth was open from a gasp.

"Rose?" Hannah asked.

"Robert no! Please don't hurt me." Rose screamed, and her image faltered and shimmered.

"Help me. Please someone help me."

Hannah clasped her hand over her mouth as Rose's image rippled like a ribbon whipped by wind.

"Oh, God, my stomach. It's burning." Rose moaned as her form dropped to the ground. It echoed eerily across the wind. "Blood, so much blood." Her voice wavered.

Hannah and Neil stopped walking. Hannah's body shook, and she shifted to run to her friend, but Neil grabbed and pulled her back.

His deep voice whispered in her ear, "Remember you're here for her. It's not real now. You have to help her."

The wind stung the wetness of her cheeks, as she cried out to Rose, "Remember Rose, I'm here. You're not alone."

"I need to get inside the car. I have to. Help me, Hannah," Rose pleaded, and she stretched toward the car.

Hannah rushed forward and knelt before the white cloud whipping in front of her.

"No, Rose. You didn't make it inside, honey. You died outside the car. You can't go in. I'm right here."

"I don't want to go, Hannah. Please don't make me go. I'm not ready," Rose pleaded in a voice that sounded like a child begging for her mom.

"It's time Rose. It's okay though. Your family is waiting for you. Do you see them?"

"Hannah?" Roses voice whispered.

"Go to your family, Rose. I'll see you some day, I promise."

"Hannah, I see them," Rose exclaimed.

"Go on. It's fine."

"Hannah, it was Robert. Tell the police he buried the knife behind the bushes over at the edge of the lot. He killed me because I wouldn't date him."

"Oh honey, I'm so sorry. I'll make sure he pays," Hannah said between the sobs that racked her. Rose's cloud vaporized along with her car. Hannah dropped her head in her hands and knelt there crying in the night. Neil dropped next to her and pulled her into his arms.

Chapter Twenty-Three

Neil pulled into the gravel driveway and parked close to the side door of his home. After opening the door and helping Hannah get out, he grabbed her bag and guided her inside. He kept his hand on her lower back and when she paused before the stairs, he waited.

"Didn't you have something to show me?" she asked.

"Not now." He placed a light pressure on her back. They proceeded upstairs and into the master bedroom. The salt lamp kept the room in a soft glow, highlighting the natural wood of the king-size bed sitting against one wall. Neil scanned the room. The dark colors suited him. But Hannah's touch would add some brightness, too.

"If you want to wash up first, we can chill here and talk about what happened," he offered. She'd need to talk it through.

"Thank you," Hannah said before disappearing into the bathroom. Neil placed her bag on the long dresser, kicked off his shoes, and sprawled on his side of the bed. His side. Her side. It had a nice ring to it. She emerged make-up free and headed toward her bag. She hadn't even paused when she noted where he waited. She grabbed her brush and ran it through her curls while toeing off her shoes. She tossed it back in her bag before joining him on the bed.

Neil wrapped his arms around her and pulled her close. She laid her head on his chest and sighed.

"How will we know if this worked? It seemed like it to me," he whispered.

"I think it did. We'll know for sure if I don't get a call tomorrow night," she answered.

He dipped his head and inhaled the scent of her hair, letting it fill him with warmth. He rubbed small circles on her lower back and kept quiet, giving her time to think about everything they'd recently experienced. After a few minutes, he whispered, "You know this Robert guy?"

Hannah's head brushed against his chest when she nodded. "Robert Larkin. I met him once during a get together one of the law students had at the beginning of the semester. He was creepy, but I never would have thought he was a killer."

"Desperate men do desperate things, honey."

"I know and it's awful," she said, before lifting herself up on one elbow and leaning over to kiss his cheek. "I'm glad you were there. Victoria said to always trust your instincts, and I feel, deep down, Rose has passed over. I'm glad for her in that way. It makes me sad to have put her through that tonight, though."

"Yeah, it was rough. But like you said, she'd blocked it and needed to experience what happened. I'm sure this time wasn't as bad as the last."

"How?" Hannah asked.

"You were there," he said, and trailed a fingertip along her chin before wrapping his hand in her hair and tugged her closer. He lightly rubbed his lips across hers, going slowly in case she wasn't ready. Her mouth pressed against his, and he took the kiss deeper. He remained on his back and let her set the pace.

Her free hand combed through his hair, and she tilted her head, slipping her tongue in his mouth. His body hardened, and Neil tightened the reins of the need ripping inside him. Heat coursed over his skin like a flame of fire tickling everywhere her body met his. His blood pounded through his veins, and he locked his body—remaining still. He could do this. She needed calm now.

Hannah slowed the kisses and eased back to rest on his chest. He fought with his lungs to soothe his breaths and keep from panting. Her breath quickened, and he squeezed his eyes shut. Calm. Inhale. Exhale. So focused on his breathing, it was a minute before he realized her breaths were slow and steady. She'd fallen asleep on him.

Women. He forced his muscles to relax and chanted a meditation to even out his own breathing. Robert Larkin, you're nailed. *Damn, I love this woman.*

Fifteen minutes later, Hannah shifted and stretched causing her breasts to crush against his chest. A moan escaped before Neil could clamp his lips shut. Fifteen minutes of her there in his arms gave him time to imagine many nights like this…and more. His body shuddered before he could lock it down. Hannah sat up, and he released a breath.

She ran her fingers through her hair and crossing her legs, rotated to face him. A small flush crept up her neck, and her lips tilted.

"I didn't mean to fall asleep."

"You needed it, obviously. Plus, it's late." Neil said, before hopping out of bed. If he didn't get farther away, he was going to jump Hannah and rip her clothes off and do everything he fantasized about during those long fifteen minutes.

Hannah scooted off the bed and tilted her head to study him. "You wanted to show me something? I'm feeling better now."

A million motorcycles gunned their engines inside his stomach. *Shit.* Times up. He dipped his head and lifted his arm.

"Downstairs. If you're up to it. We can wait until morning."

Hannah spun around and strode out of the room. Neil rushed to follow her down the steps. He'd intentionally left it dark, so when she aimed for the light switch, he slapped a hand over hers.

"Not yet," he said and placed his arms on her shoulders, guiding her to the dining room and turning her to face the kitchen. From this viewpoint, she'd be able to see everything at once. "Wait here, and I'll get the light."

Neil stepped back and using the switch in the dining room, he punched the button and a bright light flooded the kitchen—bouncing off the stainless-steel equipment poised on the counters. The glass front cabinet doors let the light inside, enhancing the dark stained solid wood interiors. One cabinet held a full set of china. The under-cabinet rack displayed four wine glasses hanging by their stems. Centered on the ceiling, hung a large pot rack where several new pots and pans hung, bouncing light around them.

Hannah gasped, and her hands covered her mouth. She skipped in and dropped her hands to trail her fingers over the wine rack, fondle the appliances, and tapped one pot—making it hit and clang against the others. Heat shot through Neil's body as she stroked one item, then the next, humming and gasping at various intervals. His mind blanked when her hands splayed on the double confectioner's oven behind her back, and she leaned back.

He shuddered and forced his mind back to Hannah. He cleared his throat.

"Well?" he asked.

Hannah faced him and grinned. "It's beautiful. All these appliances are a chef's dream. This would be my perfect kitchen." She frowned, and his stomach clenched.

"What?"

"Do you even know how to use some of these things? I mean, you never mentioned being interested in learning how to cook or even knowing how to cook."

"I don't," he said and strode up to her. Now or never. "I didn't design this kitchen for me, honey."

Her eyes widened while she scanned the kitchen quickly before turning back. "Then…who?"

"You want me to say it, don't you?"

Hannah stepped closer and looked him in the eyes to whisper, "Yes."

Neil studied the face of the woman he'd fallen in love with so long ago. His heart swelled and answered her. "I did it for you. I want this to be your kitchen."

"And?" she said with a light twinkle in her eyes.

"I want this to be your kitchen and your house with me. For the rest of our lives."

Hannah lifted herself and kissed him hard on the lips, then pulled away slightly. "I love you, Neil."

Neil's heart tripped, and he wrapped his arms around her. "I love you. Marry me."

"Yes," Hannah said, then laughed. "Yes, I'll marry you."

"Good, here," Neil said, and tugged the box he'd grabbed from the bedroom earlier and popped open the lid. The bright kitchen light caused the diamond ring to flash colors all around the room. Hannah took the ring and placed it on her finger before twirling around.

She grabbed his hand and tugged him toward the stairs, "Come on, let's celebrate."

Neil growled and chased his laughing woman up the stairs and into their bedroom where he showed her how much he loved her with his body.

****

The next morning, Hannah stretched and grinned at the soreness of her body. She rolled her head on the pillow and studied the man sleeping beside her. Her Neanderthal, her protector, her lover. She caught the aroma of cooking bacon and frowned. Neil still slept. Who was cooking?

Hannah slipped quietly from the bed and tossed on one of Neil's T-shirts. The man had to start wearing colors. Not that black wasn't sexy, but he needed some variety. She grinned. She'd help with that. She padded down the stairs and gasped. The kitchen was empty except for a soft white cloud in the center. Rose? No. A ghost? Did Neil know?

"Hello?" Hannah said to the room. Would it respond? She waited silently and cleared her mind.

"Why hello, my dear."

Hannah blinked at the southern drawl of a woman. "Can you see me?"

"Well, of course I can. It's usually the other way around, isn't it? The living being unable to see the spirits. You've had some experience in that. Rose has moved on, by the way."

Hannah tipped her head to the side, "You knew her?"

"Oh no, I didn't know her. I only know what Neil knew about her. However, I do still have some connections in this town and confirmed what I thought you might be worrying about this morning. Oh, look at that ring on your hand."

The white cloud took the shape of an older woman in a fifties style dress. A swirl of mist wrapped around Hannah's left hand, and her arm tingled from the chill.

"That man will make things proper, no doubt. I declare, you're not going to be one of those ladies who insists on waiting forevah to wed, are you?"

"Um, no. I don't want a big wedding. Something small will work for me," Hannah answered.

"How delightful. It's a shame we couldn't have met in my day. I just know the Daughters of the Magnolia State Delegate would have approved of you."

"Thank you," Hannah said. "I'm sorry, but I don't think we've met formally. My name is Hannah Lincoln."

"Oh, how dreadfully I've behaved. I must apologize. My name is Muriel Dubois Hanson, and this is Hanson House. Originally built by my dearly departed Walter."

"A pleasure to meet you. Do you know why your spirit is here?"

"Oh yes, I do. I am committed to staying at Hanson House. I have no desire to follow on into the next beyond, as others may call it. I do so hope you're agreeable to this arrangement. Neil has assured me that if I remain on the main level or in the attics, there will be no trouble."

"I'm good with that," Hannah assured Muriel. Neil's pounding feet descended the stairs.

"You didn't even give me a chance to explain first?" Neil scolded Muriel.

"Good morning, young man. I can't be blamed if you oversleep, bless your heart. I must be off then," Muriel said and evaporated.

Neil strode around the counter and grabbed Hannah, kissing her deeply, before dipping his head close to her ear and whispering, "Good morning, love."

Her body tingled where his lips touched her ear, and she trembled. Now this carried promise. She grinned and pushed him away. Clapping her hands, she whipped open the fridge, and laughed.

"What?"

"How did you know what to buy? I'd figured you for a takeout type of eater," Hannah said.

"I am. I was. Muriel helped me with the shopping list."

His face reddened, and Hannah's chest swelled. "Good for her. Sit down, and I'll fix you breakfast."

"Sounds good to me," he agreed, and sat at the counter. "By the way, before I came down I made a call. Robert Larkin will be getting picked up first thing today."

Hannah paused, then nodded. "Good."

"And," Neil said, "I have something else I need to ask you."

Hannah faced him and lifted a brow. "What is it?"

"Please tell me if you have the recipe, can you make oatmeal and cranberry cookies sometime today?"

Hannah laughed, then answered, "Of course."

"Good," Neil said, then asked, "Where do you suppose, Muriel went?"

Hannah shrugged breaking eggs in a bowl. "I don't know."

Up in the attic a white mist swirled and solidified. A brown chest slid across the dusty floor, and the locks flipped open by a small wind. One by one, various colored baby blankets floated up and over the edge. "These will need to be aired out soon," Muriel's voice sang in the emptiness.

A word about the author...

Sherrie Lea Morgan is an active member of Romance Writers of America and her local chapter Georgia Romance Writers.

She lives north of Atlanta, Georgia with her twin sister, two dogs, and two cats. When not working her current manuscripts, she enjoys spending time with her sister, daughter, and son. If time permits, she can be found watching movies that make her jump.

You can visit her at her website:
www.sherrieleamorgan.com